VALKYRIE HUNTED

ALLYSON LINDT

For my eternal dragon

CHAPTER ONE

Kirby had learned a lot over the years of training to be an assassin. At the top of that list was how predictable people were.

As she sat in a dark room with four other people, light from valley below the house on the hill streamed through the window. Mark was outside, and responsible for the power going out. She had no doubt.

Brit said she'd killed her former partner. However, despite there being two shootings in the city in the last few days, and him supposedly being one of them, a body hadn't been found. And she hadn't seen any blood after shooting him at point blank range in the chest.

Half a dozen scenarios ran through Kirby's head around what Mark's next move would be. Like so many other people, he was usually easy to read. Most things he encountered were for fucking, tormenting, or killing. And frequently, all of the above.

The lights flickered on when the backup generator kicked in.

"He's next to the house. Possibly inside." Kirby turned off the bedroom lights. No reason to make everyone a more obvious target through the windows.

"Perhaps the power simply went out." Min didn't sound like he believed his own words.

Kirby nodded at the window, and the lights glowing brightly from street lamps and other homes. "Yeah, no."

"He waited until we were all in the same room," Brit said.

That made sense. TOM had tech that allowed the user to see silhouettes through walls. Kirby didn't understand the science behind it, besides knowing it was radio-wave driven rather than thermal or infra-red. The *how* didn't matter. Mark's hunting them did.

"We have to act under the assumption he's already inside the security-camera perimeter." Starkad, her mentor and keeper, was thinking along the same lines she was. He pulled Min and Gwydion closer to the interior walls.

Kirby and Brit had already taken a similar position.

"We need to split up and fan out. He can't follow all of us at once." Kirby always had the final say in on-mission strategies. A combination of instinct and intensive training had yet to steer her wrong.

"If we leave people here, they become the primary target," Starkad said.

Which was perfect. Stationary people, especially those Mark had already spotted, were easiest to go after. He'd want to cut numbers down quickly, to increase his odds. He probably had no idea at least sixty percent of his targets were immortal. Was Kirby? She was a Valkyrie. Had recovered her wings and magical armor. She'd also regained memories of past lives, where she'd done the same and died anyway, so her survival here wasn't guaranteed.

"Unless he secured something new in the last six hours, he only has frag grenades, his M5, and probably a Desert Eagle .40." Brit ticked off the short list on her fingers.

He'd draw too much attention if he used the gear in the same city where it was purchased, even through back-channel sources. So he wouldn't have restocked.

Unless Mark wasn't thinking this through the same way they were. Just because he was looking to kill them didn't mean he'd do it by the book.

Kirby touched Min's arm. "You're a non-combatant?"

"Always."

Her memories had that right. If they really were her memories. With everything going on, the onslaught she suffered earlier seemed surreal. "Stay with Brit," she said to Min. Mark didn't have the ability to take down the god of passion. She met Gwydion's gaze next. "Your call if you'd rather stay inside or join the hunt. If you remain, we need you in a different room." He had military training, had been an army doctor, so she trusted him to know how to lay low.

"Give me a weapon." Gwydion's voice was steel.

"*Hey.*" Brit bit off the word.

Kirby finally turned to her. With the outside light falling over her pale skin and light hair, Brit looked ghostly beautiful.

Not that Kirby cared. "What?"

"You're not leaving me huddled in a corner, waiting to die. I'm never hiding from that asshole again. Give me a fucking gun."

"No." Gwydion spoke before Kirby could. "I may not have wanted to see you in pain, but you've tried to kill people in this room."

"Person. Who is apparently immortal. In fact, I'm probably the only one here who can die." She focused on Kirby. "But if I'm not, I won't lose you a third time. Not to that prick or anyone."

A fist clenched around Kirby's heart, despite her resolve to not care. Brit had tried to apologize for her past betrayals, but the things she'd said about Kirby way back when, they way Brit hung her out to dry… Those weren't the types of actions that were easily forgiven, and would never be forgotten.

"We're wasting time," Starkad barked. "Give her a gun. Fan out, staggered radial. North. South. East. West." He pointed to each of them as he handed out directions. "Brit and I will go clockwise. Kirby and Gwydion counter." He placed a finger under Kirby's chin, to raise her head and hold her gaze. "No assumptions. No bullshit."

She clenched her jaw, to bite back her retort. He was warning her to not be reckless or assume her immortality was complete or infallible. She nodded and jerked away from him, both touched that he cared and irritated he thought she'd be anything other than cautious. Then again, it had been a messy past few days.

They left Min in the middle of the house, in a pantry with multiple exits and winding hallways and counters between it and the outside entrances. If Mark chose to pursue him, it would cost him valuable time with no payoff.

Kirby headed toward her assignment, hugging the house tight with the first pass. With the tech Mark had, he couldn't tell who was who—only that there were so many bodies. Brit and Min were easy to spot in a group, with their varied height. But once the group split up, there was no good way for Mark to identify a specific person. He'd have to pick a specific target to pursue, and that meant leaving his back unguarded.

Kirby crept through the darkness, her senses on full alert. She hugged the house tight with her first circle. Why wasn't he here? The reason to take out the power would be to creep inside the perimeter of the cameras, but he hadn't.

He was drawing them out on purpose, and they were letting him. Fuck. Too late to change plans now. Apparently her instinct could fail her.

She'd been reckless in the hotel, storming out. Picking up strangers in the bar. This was real. This could be deadly. And it was as much a mission as any she'd ever been on. When she found Mark,

6

she was putting a bullet in his fucking brain. Unlike her other former classmates, he didn't have the right to ask for absolution.

The land behind the house was sweeping lawn that led to a drop-off down the side of the mountain. She stuck to the sparse brush and trees. It'd be nice to have a more controlled environment for her first real foray into *am I actually immortal?* Fate had never really favored her in that regard, though. Not in this life, and if her new memories were to be believed, not in any of the previous ones.

The crickets chirped. The traffic below was at a low roar. There were no sounds out of place.

Something small and hard pressed into the small of her back. "What does it take to make you stay dead?" Mark asked in a low growl.

How did he sneak up on her? Her stomach plummeted into her shoes. "I'd tell you, but... No, wait. I'm going to kill you either way." She didn't want to shout and draw the attention of the neighbors, but she didn't whisper either, hoping Starkad was within hearing range. Her cool demeanor was a façade, and it didn't push aside the wave of memories of every time Mark had backed her into a corner and groped her. Bruised her in practice. Reminded her she didn't do anything in that fucking school without his leave.

"You only ever had to comply. The way Brit did. The three of us would have been good together," Mark said.

Kirby didn't want to hear the words or his familiar voice. The combination tugged at years of terror she thought she'd moved past. *He'll die tonight, by my hand.* She forced the assurance to repeat in her mind, but it didn't provide comfort. "Do you really believe that?" It was an obvious question to keep him talking, but it was what she had while she thought through her options.

"Brit was happy with me. Didn't threaten me. Didn't push me away. She knew how I felt, until she saw you again. You ruined it all."

Delusional fucker. Kirby had no doubt that he'd shoot if she turned too quickly. And she didn't have any illusions about being faster than his trigger finger. Could she survive a bullet to the spine? Was she willing to bet on her immortality, to get the drop on him? She was willing to die if it meant never hearing his voice or feeling his touch again.

A gunshot rang through the night and in her ears, leaving a high-pitched whine in her head. Did he pull the trigger? She didn't feel anything. She would have at least felt a nudge, wouldn't she?

"I couldn't stand you, you fucking sociopath." Brit's voice came from behind.

Kirby knew what she'd see before she turned, but she had to look. Ambivalence speared her at the sight of Mark's lifeless body on the ground. Blood flowed from his skull, darker than the night. He was gone. Actually gone. She was seeing it with her own eyes.

But she didn't get to pull the trigger. She almost felt cheated. When she looked at Brit, any response lodged in her throat. They stared at each other, then at the body, and at each other again. It felt like an eternity, but it was only a second or two.

"Thank the gods you're all right." Starkad's voice penetrated Kirby's thoughts.

She couldn't pull her gaze from Brit.

"I need a cleanup. One body in the yard. K street. There was gunfire. He's the suspect in the last two days' events." That was Min. Who was he talking to?

Kirby needed to move. This wasn't the worst possible time for her instincts and training to fail her, but it was close.

"*Kirby*. We're going *now*." The urgency in Starkad's voice finally jarred her into action.

She shut off her emotions with one final push of disgust. "Exit options?"

"Can we leave the guns?" Brit's mind must be whirring along the same *act now, feel later* path.

"Drop them," Min said.

Kirby and Brit were trained for combat logistics, but they didn't handle clean-up. That was someone else's specialty. But Kirby did have enough sense to not take orders from random gods, regardless of what a good lay they were. Whether or not she trusted Min wasn't the question. He wasn't a combatant, and she wasn't familiar with his modern skills outside the bedroom.

She looked at Starkad, who nodded. "His info is good."

Kirby dropped her weapon, and Brit did the same. They followed Starkad and Min, away from the sirens that were growing louder.

"What about Gwydion?" Kirby didn't like the idea of leaving him behind. The cold fear that slid under her skin at the idea of something happening to him was unfamiliar and terrifying.

"He's got this—terrified neighbor who found a dead body." Starkad rested a hand on the small of her back.

Heat rushed through her, joining the jumble that was her wreck of an emotional state.

"Stay with Min. Brit is with me," Starkad said. "We have a rendezvous point. Min will give you details." He squeezed her hand once and cut in a different direction.

The gesture couldn't have been more heartfelt if he'd wrapped his arm around her waist and given her a deep, long, goodbye kiss. She hated to see him go, but for as much as she still didn't trust Brit, there were no two people Kirby felt more capable of having each other's backs than Brit and Starkad.

"A dear friend is picking us up," Min said as they strolled at a casual pace down the sidewalk. "He knows who you are, and I trust him."

She barely knew Min, aside from a clusterfuck of memories she wasn't convinced belonged to her. She was only here now because Starkad said it was safe. Trust didn't trickle down the same way. With her hair dyed, the darkness, and Gwydion's cap pulled low on her head, she wasn't easily identifiable, and that was a sliver of comfort.

As they walked through the night, emergency vehicles gathered at the house behind them. A black Porsche Cayenne that would have been pompous in a less affluent neighborhood pulled up next to them. The tension coiling inside Kirby couldn't crank higher.

The passenger window rolled down, and the man in the front seat leaned over. He looked to be in his mid-thirties. Was he really, or was he another god? Great. Kirby didn't have enough to question in her every-day life. Now she was also wondering who around her would live forever.

A memory nudged its way forward. She knew this man. He'd been with Min, both in L.A. and after World War II. Immortal, at least. His name was… on the tip of her tongue. She couldn't grasp it from her jumbled thoughts.

"You called?" His tone was conversational.

Min smiled and stepped closer. "Daz. Thank you for being available."

"Always. Are you ready?"

Kirby swore she heard a hint of affection in the man's voice. That matched her memories too. Daz adored Min.

"We are." Min opened the back door and gestured Kirby toward it.

She settled into the second row of seats, surprised and a little relieved when Min took the spot next to her. Past Kirbys didn't have any bad memories of Daz—not that were easily accessible—but she didn't feel comfortable discussing business in front of him. The way he glanced at her in the rear view mirror sent unease rolling through her.

They pulled onto the main road, and Daze maneuvered them farther from the spot where Mark's body lay.

He was dead. Never getting up. Never coming after her again. He'd thought the same of her, but she saw it with her own eyes. He was really gone.

The relief still didn't flow through her like she expected. This was a dark chapter of her life closed, and she was dwelling on the fact that she wasn't the one to carry out Mark's execution. After what Brit had told her though, Kirby didn't begrudge her the shot.

None of that quieted the screams for vengeance that echoed in her skull. Hopefully, as she moved away from threat of being caught, the tension would ebb and she could put this behind her.

"Huntress?" Min's breath teased her skin, as he pushed the loud whisper into her ear. "Are you here?"

She shook off the cobwebs of doubt. "Yes."

"Good. You need to change." He spoke in hushed tones. "If anyone outside of this car asks, you're my hired escort for the evening. I'm sorry."

She studied him in the dim light as they drove, the outside lamps splashing over his face and accentuating handsome, dark features. "For what?"

"You shouldn't have to demean yourself like that."

She leaned her head on his shoulder and turned her mouth toward his ear. "I'm already a whore. I earn my living committing immoral acts. At least getting paid for sex is honest work."

Min raised an eyebrow but didn't argue. He reached behind the seats, grabbed a duffel bag, and handed it to her. "Old clothes go in here. Hat too, I'm afraid."

Her pout slipped out without her permission. Was she actually emotionally attached to a ball cap from a guy she barely knew?

"He's got dozens. I promise you. We'll stop at a gas station, so you can change."

Kirby had already stripped off her shoes and was shoving off her jeans. "Why? Daz, if naked women bother you, keep your eyes on the road." She had a hard time fathoming that anyone who had associated with Min for this long had a problem with nudity or the human form. But Kirby swore she heard a light sigh from him. She tugged on the barely-there lace panties and bra from the stack she'd removed from the bag, and shoved her old outfit inside. The last thing in her pile of new clothing was a gold satin dress.

"Not exactly subtle." Which was perfect. She pulled it over her head. If she couldn't blend into the crowd, she needed to be the person no one wanted to make eye contact with. This was another, far more expensive, grade of the homeless costume she wore during missions.

Kirby shimmied into the dress, which fit perfectly. Almost as if it had been tailored for her. She gave Min a suspicious glance, then turned her back to him. "Zip me up, handsome?" She poured a Midwest twang into her request.

She wanted to pump Min for more information about their destination and next steps, but Daz made her uneasy. When Min tried to bring up the topic, she silenced him with a hand on his thigh and a subtle shake of her head.

When Kirby was barely a teenager, she'd been *saved* from foster care by the god Loki. He'd promised her a new home where she could learn to be a superhero, and young-Kirby loved the idea enough to ignore her cynicism.

The reality had been much darker. The Order of Mistletoe had an academy where assassins were trained, attached to their organization. Their mission was eliminating potential gods, based on a series of ancient prophecies, so the gods at TOM could retain their glory and immortality.

They framed it as *saving the world from new danger*, but Kirby had seen the truth. She just wished she'd seen it sooner. Years ago, before she was betrayed by Brit, stripped of her rank, and tried to end her own life.

These days trust was a commodity she was stingy with. It kept her alive and sane.

Less than half an hour later, Daz pulled the SUV into a municipal airport. The location eased Kirby's mind. She wasn't in the mood to deal with airport security and dozens of people. What comforted her more was walking toward the small plane with steps pushed up to it, and seeing Starkad waiting. He'd upgraded his clothing from bullet-hole filled, to a button-down shirt and slacks. *Fucking hot.*

Brit was by his side. She hadn't gotten the same tailored-gown treatment. She wore one of Kirby's T-shirts, torn intentionally, to drape off one shoulder. Her denim skirt was ripped as well, leaving the bottom edges ragged and barely covering her ass.

It would have been kind of sexy, if Kirby was in the mood to notice. Jealousy spiked through her when Brit wrapped herself around Starkad's arm and leaned into him. Brit was playing a part, and would continue to do so until she had the *all clear*. Knowing that didn't soothe Kirby.

"Thank you again," Min said to Daz.

Daz's smile almost lit up the interior of the car. "Of course. I'll park, then go talk to the pilot and ensure we're ready for flight." The moment they stepped from the SUV, he pulled away.

He didn't make it far. Three police cruisers rolled into sight, lights flashing, and blocked his path.

CHAPTER TWO

Every muscle in Starkad's body twitched from the adrenaline coursing through him. Nothing about the last couple of days had gone right, and he didn't expect the universe to start complying now. He was driving, with Brit in the passenger seat. They'd walked several blocks to a waiting car and gotten out of the neighborhood on a route the police weren't checking yet.

Brit was fidgeting. She had changed into some of Kirby's clothes, and ripped them to show off more skin. She and Kirby would play the part of *escort* for the evening, until they were in the air and clear of immediate danger.

Starkad had changed as well, into a tailored outfit that screamed *money*. He wasn't worried about his safety. A few hours ago, she shot him at point blank range. The bullets knocked him down, but that was the worst he suffered.

She and Kirby felt the brunt of the fallout. When Kirby thought he was in danger, it triggered the return of her memories from her past lives. They all spilled back at once, including the excruciating pain that came with each of her previous deaths. She'd magically inflicted that same agony on Brit.

They'd been dealing with those events when Mark ambushed the house.

Starkad would rather have Kirby by his side under all circumstances, but especially now. Not that this was a good time to talk about her recovering her past lives; she'd be as on edge as Brit was, watching their surroundings and flinching at every noise and movement.

He had Brit with him instead because he trusted Kirby, and he didn't want to let Brit out of his sight until she was on her way for good.

He was grateful she'd taken care of the Mark situation. Points in her favor.

"What are your plans for me?" Brit asked.

Get her as far from Kirby as possible and let them get on with their lives. Separately. He didn't know Brit, beyond her combat prowess and the damage she'd done to Kirby. She was another body. After so many centuries alive, he'd go mad if he let his heart bleed for every random person he encountered. "What kind of a response are you looking for?" he asked.

"If you're asking seriously, I didn't think I'd have a say in the matter, so I haven't given it any consideration. If you want my facetious, off-the-cuff answer, give me twenty grand and drop me in Paris."

"Done."

Brit scoffed. "What?"

"I can have traveler's checks and a new ID waiting for you in Paris. From there, you're on your own." It sounded like a best-of-all-worlds solution to Starkad. That should make him nervous, but he couldn't afford to second-guess everything.

"What's the catch?" Suspicion lined Brit's question.

No catch, just one requirement. "You don't go looking for Kirby. Ever."

Silence stretched through the car. Out of the corner of his eye, he saw Brit fiddle with the newly frayed edges on her skirt.

"Deal." She didn't sound so certain.

He wasn't giving her a chance to change her mind. Fortunately, they were at the municipal airport. He parked and joined Brit in front of the car. They were the first ones here, as was the plan. He'd have a hard time standing still until Kirby and Min arrived.

Brit fell into her role easily, and he did the same, pasting on the happy mask of a guy who was going to get his money's worth from his *date* tonight.

Another vehicle approached the private hanger, and Brit tensed against him. He couldn't be wound any more tightly without shattering.

The high-end SUV stopped, and Min helped Kirby out. She was wearing gold satin that hugged every curve, and showed off how stunning and honed her body was. Her gaze flicked over him and Brit, and a frown crossed her face before she let Min wrap an arm around her waist.

Red and blue flashed in a slow strobe over the area, and Starkad clenched his fist. Police. He should have expected that.

Three cop cars skidded to a stop, blocking the ground exit and the runway.

If there were any group he'd choose to be with when he was surrounded by police, it was this one. The thought wasn't comforting.

Three officers stepped from their vehicles, all of them with their hands hovering near their holstered weapons. The man in front focused on Starkad. "Evening, sir. I'm sorry about the delay. We've had some trouble in the area over the last couple of days and since you filed this flight plan in the last hour, we have a few questions for you before you take off. Once we're done, you can be on your way."

Some trouble was an interesting way to phrase *two shootings downtown in the last few days, and a murder less than an hour ago.*

Starkad made sure to keep an appropriate amount of disdain on his face and nodded at Min. "It's my buddy's plane." He pushed a waver into his voice. "You'll have to talk to him."

The officer raised his eyebrows, and his colleagues moved their hands nearer to their weapons. "Can I see some ID, sir?" Officer One didn't sound so friendly, as he addressed Min.

Min raised both hands to shoulder level. "It's in my front jacket pocket. I can grab it, or you can."

Officer Two drew his gun and leveled it at Min. The tension on the airstrip was almost tangible, and most of it radiated from the police. Starkad hid his twisted amusement, as Officer One drew closer, his gaze never leaving Min. The guy had no clue that, if Kirby deemed him a threat, he was dead the instant his firearm was within her reach.

Since she'd ascended, she didn't technically need the gun, but she might not know that yet. And he'd never, across any life, seen her use a Valkyrie's power to take life off the battlefield. For this Kirby, if she thought someone was going to open fire, this *was* a battlefield, and whoever took the first shot had initiated the war.

Officer One grabbed Min's wallet, and nearly dropped it again in his haste to step back. His eyes grew wide when he opened the leather trifold and a stack of cash greeted him. He thumbed over the wallet contents, then extracted a business card and a driver's license. He looked between them and Min. "Is this you?"

"Yes, sir."

"I'm sorry to have wasted your time." Officer One shoved everything back in twice as fast as he'd withdrawn it, and handed Min's wallet back. "You and your... friends have a lovely evening."

Min's smile grew. "Thank you, officer. Do *you* have a business card or phone number? I'd like to let your chief know what a pleasure it was speaking with you this evening."

Officer One fumbled in his own wallet and finally retrieved a card that he handed to Min.

Starkad bit the inside of his cheek, to hold back the laughter. He'd forgotten how much fun it was to see Min throw the weight of his company name around. Especially in response to prejudice and assumption.

With the police gone, Starkad and the others boarded the plane. There was minimal conversation while they prepped for takeoff and taxied down the runway.

When they were in the air, Kirby looked between Min and Starkad. "Can we...?"

"Speak freely? Yes," Starkad said.

Kirby was tense. It wasn't obvious, but after so many years with her, he knew how tightly coiled her body was under the calm facade. "Where's Gwydion?"

She'd asked for Gwydion first when she woke up after recovering her memories, too. A fact that still gnawed at Starkad. He expected things to be tense between them when her past came back to her—Starkad had kept her at arm's length physically for years. Much to her dismay and his discomfort.

Starkad had his reasons for not fucking her, but that didn't mean Kirby would see things that way when he had a chance to explain. "He stayed behind to deal with the police, and hasn't shared any other plans with me."

"I see." She frowned.

"Though, whatever he's doing probably involves making his way back to you." Starkad wouldn't withhold that knowledge out of jealousy, regardless of temptation.

The corners of Kirby's mouth tugged up, but she stopped the smile before it formed. She focused on Min. "I thought I knew who you were. After that cop's reaction to your wallet, I'm thinking there are still secrets."

"You don't remember." Min frowned.

Frustration flashed across her face.

"*I* don't remember." Brit huffed. "I have no idea what ninety percent of this is. Why did Officer Friendly look like you could destroy his world with your thumb? Does your business card say *Big Mighty God* on it?"

Min tossed her the wallet. She'd find the same thing the officer did—that Min was president of one of the largest investment companies in the world. His money had been behind ventures that connected people to the internet back when it was new, and more recently, the biggest social media platforms.

Brit twisted her mouth when she landed on the ID and business card, and she handed the wallet back.

"I do remember. A… pool." Kirby trailed off.

Min tucked his wallet away again. "And you remember sunbathing naked in it? The L.A. riots?"

The color drained from Kirby's face, and she nodded slowly. "It's all real, isn't it? Everything tucked in my head."

"Yes." Starkad couldn't fathom how much her mind was trying to process. He had a hard enough time holding onto the last few decades, and her entire history of thirteen lives had been shoved back into her head at once.

Kirby rubbed her palms up her face, then dragged them back down again, a long sigh escaping through her fingers. She stood and walked from the passenger cabin of the plane.

Silence settled in again.

"Will she be all right?" Brit asked softly.

Starkad had been asking himself that for far too long. He went in search of Kirby. Fortunately, no matter how nice the place was, it was still a plane cruising at 45,000 feet, and she didn't have many places to go. Technically, she could fly with her summoned wings, but they would have noticed the cabin depressurizing if she'd stepped out the door mid-flight.

He found her in the next room, thumbing through mini liquor bottles secured behind the bar.

She extracted one with a deep amber label, and set it on the bar top. "Brit's being awfully quiet. No demands. No accusations. No self-righteous indignation."

That was one piece of news he could get out of the way quickly. "She and I talked on the way here. She's going her own way, complete with a promise to not pursue you."

"You talked without me?" Kirby fiddled with the bottle, clanking the plastic against the counter. "Which makes sense. It's her life. Her decision." Her agreement didn't erase the conflict from her expression. "I want to ask you so many things, but I don't know where to start."

"Pick one. We'll go from there."

Kirby shook her head. "I've said too much already. Today. In the past. So have you. Things that can't be taken back, and can't be healed by a series of past lives that look more to me like a vivid movie than memories."

"Are we done speaking, then?" He'd fight a decision like that. But she was as addicted to him as he was to her. She'd never made a secret of it.

"I don't know," Kirby said.

Starkad brushed his fingers over the back of her hand. She jerked back as if she'd been shocked. A stony mask slid in quickly, and she leaned back against the far wall. That hurt.

"I'll answer the question you asked when you woke up," he said.

Why? That was the only thing she'd said to him the first time she regained consciousness after becoming a Valkyrie again.

"I don't even know what it was in reference too. Everything I can't vocalize now, I suppose. And I swear to Freya, if you say—"

"I was just doing what I thought was best?"

She scowled. "Yeah. That."

"I'm not going to say it." Starkad had beaten that phrase to death, and he didn't believe it himself anymore.

"I don't know what to tell you. What to ask."

Starkad ached to cross the divide between them. To lift her chin and gaze in her eyes. To fall into what they were in their first life. Before curses and immortality and losing her so many times.

But they'd never have that again. They could have something better, or their romantic relationship could be dead in the water.

"I loved you so much when you were Ruby," he said. "What you did for me? I would have done the same for you and more, without hesitation." He was a berserker. A warrior who had fought for his god and his faith without question, and centuries ago had died a glorious death on the battlefield.

Kirby had been the Valkyrie he loved. She stopped one of her sisters from takin him to Valhalla, defying Odin, and had given Starkad immortality to ensure they'd always be together.

As punishment for her insubordination, Odin cursed her to be reborn and die again and again.

"You would have done the same for her. Not me. And you did. It's why you were on that battlefield."

Not quite, but close. Odin had been her god. Her master. And Starkad served the Allfather because she did. Starkad had fought in any battle he could find, regardless of the cause; he'd been made for war. As had Kirby. Once he met the Valkyrie and fell in love, he chose his sides for her. "It's true."

She crossed her arms, hugging herself. "What would you have done if you found Brit in the bottom of that shower, instead of me?"

She'd fast-forwarded to this life, when he'd found her nearly dead after she slit her own wrists. Not enough time had passed to diminish the terror he felt that night, when he saw her on the shower floor, blood caked to her skin and clothes, her skin as pale as the white tile she sat on.

It was his fault she'd been with TOM. He refused to extract her when they recruited her at thirteen. He'd told Min and Gwydion it was the best place for her to learn to defend herself. The only way to keep her from dying again.

Starkad never expected the experience to break her.

"I've told you, she's nothing to me," Starkad said. "She was a student who registered on my radar because you cared. I kept contact with her because she reached out to me with information about how to get back at TOM. If I'd found her there, I would've called for a campus doctor. I would have mourned her life if she didn't survive and her sanity if she did. And I would have grieved for you in your pain."

"You weren't saving me that day. You were saving *Ruby*." Bitterness spilled from Kirby.

Starkad wished he could argue. He was tired of the half-truths and misdirection. "It's true. But I know *you* now. What I do, all of it, is for the woman I love—you." He'd tried to hard to keep is distance, even after he saved her. But living so closely with her, seeing the fierce soldier mingled with the passionate woman, he couldn't help but give her his heart again.

"Fuck you." She choked out the words. "You don't get to say that, after denying it for so long. And don't you dare tell me you were doing any of this to keep me safe. I would hurt a lot less right now if I were dead. You did this for you."

Another truth he wished he could deny. "I did a lot for selfish reasons—all having to do with keeping you in my life and alive. I won't apologize for that. I'm only sorry for one thing."

She raised an eyebrow and met his gaze.

"I'm sorry I pushed you away. I thought, if I didn't love you—if I resisted the pull—it wouldn't hurt so much when you died again."

"*When*. Not *if*." She'd caught his slip. "Surprise. I'm not going anywhere in this life. I'm done dying."

26

He hoped that was true. He prayed for it on a regular basis, to any god who would listen. "Then we're in uncharted territory."

"So... what next?" She stepped closer and rested her palms on the bar.

Impulse and desire overwhelmed him. He leaned in to grip her hair, and crushed his mouth to hers. He poured his soul into the connection—his love and need, every single time he'd held back since meeting her. With a counter between them, it put them off balance. Kirby whimpered and gripped his arms, digging in her fingers to hold herself upright.

The kiss soothed Starkad's heart and quieted the chatter in his mind.

Kirby broke away first, a cool mask in place. "A kiss doesn't change anything. I fucking wanted you. I was desperate for you to notice me. To fuck me. To love me. But knowing what I do? What you kept from me? You're going to have to earn everything."

"That's fair." Not that he wouldn't push hard to make things right between them. "Until then, I'm still you keeper." They did have a job to do.

"Yes. And I trust you with my life. But you can't have my heart. Not yet. What's the plan?"

He should have expected this. Every time he'd pushed her away, this was her response. To slide into business. To box up her heart. He couldn't demand she love him, though. "We're going home. Mission is over."

"We're what? In other words, we're pretending my entire world wasn't destroyed in the last twenty-four hours?"

"What would you rather do?" He almost took the question back. If her answer was the same as Brit's *give me cash and set me free*, he couldn't comply so easily. But it was Kirby's choice, and it was probably safer for her. "You can have the same option as Brit. If you walk away now, I'll give you whatever you ask for and wish you a nice existence."

"That would make you miserable."

Or worse. "Yes."

"It's tempting."

"To make me suffer?"

Kirby shrugged. "It's tempting, but it's not what I want. I want to drive TOM into the ground, head first. Obliterate Hel and Loki, and watch that fucking institution crumble." Venom spilled out with the words, and blackness flickered around her, devouring the light for a moment.

"It's not that easy." He knew. He'd been working on the details longer than she'd been in this body.

She pursed her lips. "I figured there was a reason you hadn't done it already."

"What you've been doing is part of a bigger picture. It helps—"

"Stop." Kirby fiddled with one of the bottles. "What I've been doing is sitting on my ass, waiting for the next order, and complying. I don't know anything about the Followers of Urd except that they're working to stop TOM from stopping a series of prophecies that may or may not leave the world a better place once they've all come to pass."

She twisted the lid, breaking the seal, but didn't uncap the bottle. She tapped the plastic cap against her bottom lip. "And I've never been cryptic about what I want—you, and to see TOM fall. Though, that first one…"

Her backing off, not pushing for sex or anything romantic, was what Starkad had been trying to convince her was best for years. Now that she was surrendering, he hated it. *Careful what you wish for.*

"As long as you're here, so am I," he said. "Until we figure out what we are or aren't. But why now? I mean, this desire to pursue TOM more intently." He wouldn't try to talk her out of destroying TOM, because it had been his goal for years. He understood the drive; she'd suffered a lot at their hands.

"The instant Brit and Mark asked for permission to hunt me, they confirmed for TOM that I was alive. I can't hide anymore."

There was more to it than that. He let silence lapse between them, to see if she would offer anything else.

She stared back, jaw set and mini bottle clenched in her hand. "Call it a moment of clarity. Maybe reliving so many deaths has made me less eager for another one. Life looks different now. Not better, just a more distinct shade of bleak. I…" She sighed. "It's always been easier to not ask too many question. To accept your answers and pretend the only thing that exists is the little bubble we live in. Knowing what I do now, what you've kept from me—who those other Kirbys were, and that Urd and TOM are so much bigger than I realized—I can't ignore the rest of the world anymore."

Starkad never meant to shelter her. TOM was supposed to be the opposite of that. But if he looked at things through her eyes, he could see how much he'd cut her off from life. "All right."

"Really?"

He nodded. "It won't be an easy execution— either the plan or their deaths. I've been trying to discover how to destroy Hel for years. But if you'd like to be a bigger part of it, all right."

"No exceptions? No *you can do this, but not that*?"

"I suppose it depends on the situation, but none of the type you're talking about." It would be odd, not hiding anything from her. A habit he'd have to work to break. But honesty was the least he could offer. "I'm not willing to test your immortality, for instance." He could jab her, to see how quickly she healed. But Gwydion did that with her in Kuwait almost thirty years ago, and she'd still died from a bullet to the heart. "I trust you to be as cautious as you always have been." Maybe a little more, considering her self-destructive tendencies.

This was going to make her more reckless, and the notion hurt.

Kirby tossed him the liquor bottle, which he snagged out of the air without pause. She stepped around the bar to join him, and brushed her lips over his so lightly, he wasn't sure he felt it. "Thank you," she said softly.

"For?"

"Trying." She turned and strode toward the main room.

Starkad would take that for now. And when this was all over, they'd figure out where they belonged.

Hopefully, it was *together*.

CHAPTER THREE

Brit needed to talk to Kirby. To finish the conversation Mark's attack interrupted. Knowing gods existed was part of everyday life; Brit had been raised by them.

Finding out her ex-girlfriend was alive, was the last remaining Valkyrie, and had somehow earned the favor of at least two gods and whatever Starkad was… Brit struggled to process it. And she only had a few more hours to make something about her past with Kirby right, before they went their separate ways.

Min and Starkad were on the far side of the cabin, swapping stories about the past that had them laughing sometimes and scowling others.

Kirby had earphones in and was staring out the window.

Brit sat down across from her.

Kirby met her gaze but didn't take out the earbuds.

Brit raised an eyebrow. She wasn't going to talk to someone who couldn't hear her, and she refused to shout.

Kirby rolled her eyes and plucked out the buds. "I'm all talked out. Especially when it comes to my past."

"What about my past?"

"I'm not really interested in hearing again how your life is all my fault and I'm a monster for looking out for you."

Brit winced at both the reminder and the bitterness in Kirby's retort. She'd apologized for the things she said during Kirby's trial, but with all that came after, the new words apparently hadn't left the same impression as the old. "I—" Her thoughts were jumbled, and she didn't know how to sort them. "Mark told me you'd be okay after the hearing. That you'd get a slap on the wrist, at the most. He said I'd suffer so much worse than I already had, though. And that was saying a lot."

"You weren't the only one who put up with his shit. I took it for years, thinking it was keeping him away from you. And I never resented you for it. I never betrayed you."

"I'm not you. I'm weak. A coward." Brit spat the words. She didn't need Kirby's reminders about any of the above.

Kirby grasped Brit's fingertips and held her gaze. "You're not weak; you're selfish. You're insecure." She tightened her grip until Brit's fingers throbbed with the pressure.

Brit resisted the urge to pull away, focusing on the hurt and disbelief inside, instead. She fumbled through her anger for a protest.

"You were the best sniper TOM had." Kirby stared her down, applying consistent pressure to her knuckles and fingertips. "You're better than me. And you were beaten down for years by a system and a man that fucked us both over. Since I left, I've tortured myself so much worse than they ever did. I have a teensy idea of what you're going through. I still never betrayed you."

Brit yanked her hand away. "I get it. I was a piece of shit. I wished the instant I said anything, way back then, that I could take it back."

"You could have. Right then. You could have backtracked at any point before they escorted me out of the hearing. Or for the next twelve hours, while I sat in my room, staring blankly at the wall and wondering if I really was the monster you painted me as. If I'd really been so dim that I missed all the signs that you loathed me so completely. I compared myself to Mark."

Bile rose in Brit's throat, as regret mixed with self-defense. "I'm sorry." The apology carried more of an edge than she intended.

"Me too." Kirby leaned back in her seat. "That you did it. Not that it happened."

Brit didn't know how to respond. The jab of hurt in her lungs stole her breath and voice.

"We'd both still be there if it hadn't," Kirby said. "And I'd still think you loved me."

"I—"

"Don't." Kirby palmed her earbuds. "You're looking for me to either absolve you or hate you, so you can blame your actions on me some more. I won't give you either one." She plugged her ears again.

Fury and frustration spilled through Brit. She wanted to rip out Kirby's earphones and pursue this conversation. To scream and yell. To find closure. Kirby owed her that, gods damn it.

After Starkad rescued Kirby from TOM, she dealt with nightmares. Horrific dreams that would wake her up screaming in terror. And that was if they let her sleep at all. Her solution was cutting. The cool, soothing slice of a razor on her skin offered an external distraction, and a rush of endorphins that came with the pain.

Until Starkad found out. He'd offered a different solution—teaching her how to appreciate and respect the pain rather than abuse it. His lessons came with spanks and lashes to her backside, and she'd reveled in the delicious agony.

His only rule was that it never lead to sex. When she demanded he break that rule, the sessions ended. It had hurt so much at the time. A new kind of pain and rejection, worse even than when Brit turned on her.

Kirby needed something else to do with her mind and her body, so she'd asked to be let into other parts of his life.

He'd introduced her to TOM's opposite. The Followers of Urd. Urd was the sister of fate who wrote the original prophecies. The quintets that seemed to drive the lives and decisions of so many gods, especially Hel and Loki and everyone else associated with TOM.

Starkad explained that FU made sure life was allowed to happen, prophecies or otherwise, without interference.

When Kirby discovered that meant dismantling TOM, one assassin at a time, she didn't need any more information. From that point on, it was easier to go with the flow than to push for more information. Starkad told Kirby where each job was, and she followed. She scouted the mission area and made most of the decisions about the job itself

As she sat on Min's private jet, listening to him and Starkad discuss the next steps to eliminate Hel, she wished she'd asked more questions sooner. Being involved in planning where to go and how to get there was a new experience for her.

She agreed with most of what was proposed, mostly out of lack of knowledge. The one argument she had was when they wanted her to go to London with Min, while Starkad met Gwydion in Norway. She kept the thought to herself, though. Her only reason for protest was the newness of this all. This was what she'd asked for though, and she got it.

She didn't realize how much it would ache to watch Starkad step toward the exit of the plane without her, in Norway. She wanted to kiss him and slap him and turn her back, pretending she didn't care. Instead, she said, "Tell Gwydion I'm sorry I lost his hat." She was such an idiot.

Starkad squeezed her hand. "I will. We'll see you soon."

That would have to do. Brit disembarked with him. He was making good on their deal, and putting her on a separate flight to Paris from here. Brit gave Kirby one final glance, and this time, Kirby turned away without so much as a facial twitch.

Now what? The need to be alert that always hummed through her veins was louder than normal, as the plane took to the air again. She wanted to interrogate Min, to maybe make sense of her thoughts. But she was also burned out on the heart-to-hearts that had no resolution. She slumped in her seat instead.

He took the spot across from her, filling the space with both his presence and his size. "You're on edge."

"Usually." This wasn't her looking to forget the world and get laid, or hiding in some safe house while plans were put in motion. Was this life now? At least for the near future? In the past, between hunts, she'd read and game and live in that little world she was leaving behind. Was there such a thing as *between hunts* anymore?

"What can I do, to put you at ease?"

She shook her head. "If I knew that, I'd have indulged a long time ago. What are you looking for, from me?" Not that she'd comply *just because,* but she was curious.

"I suppose that remains to be seen. I'd like to start with getting to know you."

"No offense, but I'm super burned out on soul searching right now. Apparently my ghosts have ghosts."

"We have time." There was a pause in his words, as if he didn't quite believe them.

She wasn't in the mood to call him on it. For as many times as past versions of her died in front of him, his hesitation made sense. "I suppose we do."

"May I ask you something?"

As long as it didn't require any soul-searching. "Sure."

"The woman at the house, who disembarked with Starkad, she was a former lover of yours?"

Kirby swallowed the bile that rose in her throat. "Yes."

"The man who came to the house, whom she left dead for the police, he had been her partner?"

"Yes." How long could she get away with the one-word answers? "And she thought she killed him, before she went after Starkad. She was wrong." There. Now she'd offered more information. It needed to be enough.

The sympathy in Min's gaze wasn't comforting. "Do you have any idea why she tried to kill him?"

"Yes."

Min's lips drew into a thin line.

"Mark was an obsessive sociopath, who convinced Brit to turn on me, and who made both of our lives a literal hellscape. And in the end, he thought he was doing it for love." Kirby spat out the words. "Is that the answer you're looking for? He tortured us, through our teen years, because he

38

thought that was affection, and if she hadn't gotten to him first, I would have emptied my magazine into his skull and reloaded to make sure the job was done." She snapped her jaw shut, wincing at her own loss of control.

"I'm sorry." Min sounded genuine.

She didn't want his pity. "Me too."

"We'll change the subject. What do you do to pass the time with Starkad?"

She studied Min. How much did he know about the past few years of her life? Another question, for another time. She'd spilled too much tonight, and was grateful for the new subject. "I read. He travels a lot. We game when he's home." They'd been getting closer, but that fell apart when she demanded sex he wasn't prepared to give.

Min handed her a tablet. "Feel free to read whatever you'd like. I'm here to talk, if you'd prefer."

"Thank you." She tried to keep the kindness in her reply. She was grateful for all he'd done for her up to this point, but her mind was someplace else.

Perspective could be amazing, or it could be horrific. Today it allowed her to stand on the other side of the chasm that had split between her and Starkad, and stare into the void in between.

That sucked.

Kirby was used to waking up in strange beds, but not usually in hotels this nice. Okay, not ever. Her room was white and cream and had gold and high-thread-count sheets that were softer than satin against her skin.

Life with Starkad was modest. She'd always suspected he had more money than he let on, but it wasn't hers, and she was grateful he took care of her. Traveling with Min was vastly different, and she'd only been doing it for a day, a portion of which she'd slept through.

She climbed from the bed and yanked on some clothes. When they'd landed in London, there was luggage waiting for her in the hotel. Min told her Daz had made the arrangements. It was only a couple of days' worth of clothing and essentials, but Min promised to take her shopping for more when she was ready.

The sweater and jeans fit her perfectly. Was she the same size as other Kirbys? How odd was it that she'd had the same name in every life? Another side effect of Odin's curse. Ought to make her easier to find, at least with modern technology. Was that how she'd been picked up in this life when she was so young? But Starkad hadn't come for her. Loki had.

More questions to add to the growing list, crowding its way out of her skull. With a little sleep between the implosion of her universe and now, she could make more sense of all the things she needed to. It was still a lot, and she wasn't sure where to start, but being able to think through some of it helped.

She padded from the bedroom, to find Min in the main room of the hotel suite. When they'd arrived, he didn't blink at her request for a separate bed. Her memories said he insisted on devotion. That he required she give her all to their love, and that he would do the same in return.

Would she have thrown away a thousand years, looking for him, if he was the one who died over and over? Trying to decipher the answer through layers of denial and memories of intense love made her throat ache, so she shoved the thought into the same box as all the others.

He looked up from his laptop, giving her his full attention. "How did you sleep?"

The question caught her off guard. It shouldn't. That was a nice, polite thing, that normal people talked about. She spent a lot of time trying not to think about how she slept, though. "All right, I suppose." The last few days must have caught up to her, because she remembered her head hitting the pillow, and then nothing else. That was nice, and something she never achieved without drugs.

A surge of fear rose in her throat. She'd been unconscious and completely unaware, with a near-stranger. She swallowed the reaction. Starkad wouldn't have sent her off with Min if the god couldn't be trusted.

Starkad has made a lot of bad decisions when it comes to me. "I don't love you, you know." Kirby cringed. Where the fuck did that come from?

"I understand." Min gestured to the seat across from him. "Join me. I can have food brought up." He was taking this all in stride.

Kirby wished she could. She crossed the room and settled on the couch perpendicular to Min's. The leather was soft, embracing her. "Food sounds good. Are you going to tell me what my favorite dish is?"

"Not unless you'd like me to. I don't how accurate I'll be."

She relaxed a little. She wasn't the only one feeling her way through this. "I don't want anything elaborate. Fruit, maybe?" On second thought... "Or maybe not. Hotel fruit isn't always great."

He smiled. "I don't think you'll be disappointed." He called down a room-service order and turned back to her.

She was too drained still, to flirt or make get-to-know you conversation. "How are things looking?" This part of their plan had been vague. Min said they might be able to find answers here, but that he couldn't arrange the rest until they landed. She left her question open ended, to give her an idea of how in-depth his information-sharing skills were.

"I have a friend who owns a bookstore a few blocks from here. He's got a copy of the same book of prophecy that TOM draws their information from." Min clicked a few times on his laptop, then turned the screen toward her.

The building he showed her was gorgeous. Stone facing, with books filling the front windows. "May I?"

He nodded.

She pulled the computer closer and used the address as a jumping off point, to search for more information about the area. Photos of surrounding businesses and alleys. Floor plans. "There are a lot of copies of the prophecies." Starkad had three different volumes that were always on the shelves of whatever house they ended up in long-term. Not that she ever touched them. She got enough of that in school. TOM, drilling the important notes into her head. Telling her how the world would end in ice and snow if they didn't destroy potential gods.

"This is a copy of the original wood engraving, passed down over the centuries. It's not the original prophecies, of course, because those came to be before written language. This was the first time someone wrote it all down. It contains his notes. Thoughts. Interpretations. All of it. It's not something he lets out of his hands."

She didn't look up from her research. "The original? Do you speak Old Norse?" Wouldn't it make more sense for Starkad to be here?

"No. But you do."

The simple statement chilled her. She paused, fingers hovering over the keyboard. "I don't." Those other Kirbys did.

"There's a photo of one of the pages," he said. "In the task bar. Feel fortunate—I believe this is the ever time he's photographed the book."

Kirby hesitated. This was ridiculous. She had these memories. They had to come from somewhere. Why was there a tremor of fear, at the idea of confirming they belonged to her? And why didn't she like the way this fear tasted? In the past, fear had always been delicious and tempting. She opened the image. None of the writing looked familiar. It might as well be scribbles.

"As you are, for all of time..." She trailed off as the words rolled from her tongue. "I can read it."

"You sound disappointed."

"No. I'm…" She didn't want to admit she was afraid. This wasn't a rational feeling. Then again, nothing about this experience was reasonable or something she could have anticipated.

A knock interrupted, saving her from having to finish the sentence, and Min left to answer. He returned a moment later with the waiter, and Kirby's tension cranked in a new direction. What was Min doing, letting a random stranger into their room, without vetting him first? She swallowed the desire to shout the question but didn't take her eyes off the man with the food.

Did he look familiar? Ridiculous question. He was blond, with a medium build and height. He looked like half the country. He pushed the cart to the spot Min indicated, near a table a few meters away.

No, he definitely looked familiar.

You're being paranoid.

Her instinct was never wrong, and paranoia kept her alive.

He gestured to the various dishes on the tray. Fresh melon, berries, and plums. Min was right; it did look good. The waiter's movements were fluid and practiced.

Which made sense if he did this dozens or hundreds of times a day. But the glide of his hand was too smooth. Too deliberate.

Kirby did recognize him. He'd been a student when she was promoted. As she got older, she didn't spend much time in student teaching—that was for cadets, and privates who didn't make the field cut. But this guy…

He'd be a lot older than the last time she saw him. That would explain her not recognizing him right off.

Still paranoid.

She was right about him. She had to be. Her pulse hammered in her ears, as she tracked his every movement. Words were exchanged, but she didn't register them.

The waiter glanced at her and winked. He grabbed the steak knife near one of the plates, gripping the handle tight, and drew his arm back. He was going to attack.

CHAPTER FOUR

Gwydion had never really been off the radar. He didn't go out of his way, to hide his presence from the other gods. TOM didn't care for him, but that was based more on a thousand-year-old grudge, from a time when his believers destroyed theirs other on battlefields, to solve their differences. A time when the Vikings discovered the isles for the first time, and the Celts didn't care for the way they introduced themselves.

But Gwydion hadn't gone out of his way to piss off any of the Norse pantheon in a while. Setting foot in their territory after helping to rip away a piece of their organization felt like taunting them.

He strolled down the sidewalk with Starkad. The buildings here were mostly older—stone structures he remembered from a century ago, when he was last here—but a handful of modern buildings dotted the landscape. It was surreal. Anyone who said fictional worlds were more magical than real ones didn't appreciate what a still-populated ancient city held.

"Are you going to say it?" Starkad asked.

Since they met up at their hotel a few hours ago, the conversation had been mostly about planning. Dry but necessary.

Gwydion didn't understand the new direction. "Say what?"

"*I told you so.*"

Gwydion had been tempted a few times. This incarnation of Kirby was disconcerting. But in a lot of ways he didn't like to look at too closely, he connected with her more than ever. "Nope."

"Because you're the bigger man?"

Too easy. "Thicker, not longer."

Starkad pinched the bridge of his nose. "Wonderful. Thank you for reminding me there are less mature things than a room full of thirteen-year-olds."

"Which you never enjoyed a single second of." Bitterness slid into Gwydion's retort without his permission.

"And there it is." Starkad steered them down a side street. The decision had been made to split the teams up this way because Starkad and Gwydion knew the contact here, and Min needed someone with him who could read the book his friend had.

Gwydion suspected Starkad was happy to separate him from Kirby. It had to sting, that she asked for Gwydion's company first, after her memories came back. Not that he was smug about it. Only a lot. "She knows how to survive. She's the ultimate TOM specimen, and she's not theirs." Gwydion was falling short with the reassurances. Probably because they were bullshit.

"Perfectly honed, down to the obsession, depression, and PTSD." Starkad easily navigated the back streets.

"She's alive." Gwydion had zero complaints there. "We can't change the past, as we all know too well, and she came out the other side intact." They just had to keep her that way.

"I never had any contact with her, outside of instruction, when we were with TOM. I never introduced myself when she was younger, and I kept my distance until I pulled her out."

Pulled her out. Starkad never explained the circumstances that led him to make the decision when he did, but Gwydion had seen the scars on the inside of Kirby's wrists and the fainter ones along her chest. He recognized the same haunted look that stared back at him in the mirror almost daily, even before her past had rushed back to torment her. "You don't have to justify yourself to me."

"I have to justify myself to me."

Gwydion wasn't his priest. He didn't want to hear a confession that was about a circumstance of Starkad's own making. "Take it up with your own gods, then. Oh wait. They've forsaken you."

"Fuck you."

Was this fun—pushing Starkad's buttons? "Pretty sure that's more of a threat to you than me. You're the one beating yourself up over this."

"Kirby's not too happy about it either."

It wasn't fun. Turned out taking jabs at Starkad was kind of like kicking a puppy. A big, adorable, rip-his-throat-out-without-hesitation puppy. "She's alive. She's out now. She has the chance to make her own decisions, and none of her lives has been easy. This one has been the most scarring"—Gwydion couldn't help the dig—"but she was in the foster-care system before TOM found her. You can't say the alternative would have been better or worse."

They stepped through a door that looked like all the rest of the generic steel entrances in the alley, and the noise of the world vanished behind them. There was a unique energy in here, faint but lined with ages of wisdom. Threatening to those it didn't care for. But Gwydion liked the way it flowed over and around him.

The stone ground had seen millions of feet in its lifetime, but it was firm under theirs. They strolled a short distance to another door, this one wooden, and Starkad pushed inside.

It was like stepping into another universe. Leather and wood and iron decorated the walls and shelves. The cautious energy was stronger in here. Gwydion smiled at the familiarity of it all. He didn't care for most gods of war, but this one was an exception.

Two cats wound their way around his legs but hissed at Starkad.

"Girls, leave the wolf alone." A woman stepped from behind a fur curtain that cut the back room off from the main shop. Her age was impossible to determine—somewhere between twenty and sixty based on appearance alone. Her pale hair hung in dreadlocks around her shoulders, and her loose dress hinted at the strong body beneath. She clapped, and the cats scattered back to the shadows. "Gentlemen." Freya approached and pulled Starkad into a brief hug. She offered Gwydion the same. "It's been too long."

Gwydion shrugged. "You need to come visit me sometime. My door's always open."

"And where are you this year?" Freya asked.

Fair question. Gwydion tended to be a nomad.

She leaned against a nearby counter and gave her attention to Starkad. "I'm surprised it took you so long to seek me out."

"Why?" Surprise splashed across his face.

"Your Valkyrie. You have her again."

Gwydion swallowed his thoughts. It was tempting to pull out a funny quip, but with his current mood, it might come out more as bitter.

"I wouldn't say I *have* her," Starkad said. "Rather, I do know where she is. How did you...?"

"She's never told you."

Starkad raised an eyebrow. "Obviously."

Gwydion would enjoy Starkad's being left in the dark, if he wasn't as well.

The corner of Freya's mouth tugged up. "She prays to me. Has for years."

The notion of Kirby praying to anyone was foreign to Gwydion. In most of her lives she'd been drawn to religion, but in this one, she didn't seem big on putting her faith in anything she couldn't see.

Prayer didn't work the way most people thought. The god heard the sentiment if prayers were sent in faith, but it was more of a feeling or a whisper, than a distinct set of words. Unless the plea flowed on a massive force of will, a god didn't respond beyond sending a nudge of comfort. For most of them, it was more of a subconscious response.

"I didn't know. I'm glad she has that." Starkad almost sounded relieved.

"Is she the reason you're here?" Freya asked.

Starkad was grateful to cut through the small talk, to get to the point. He enjoyed spending time with the goddess, but he was wound too tightly to appreciate idle chatter. "Indirectly. She remembers who she is, and that prompted the visit, but we're here for a different reason."

"Join me." Freya gestured toward another room.

They followed her. Starkad was almost certain Freya had stepped in when Kirby tried to kill herself. He was also glad she hadn't said anything about *his* prayers.

Gwydion was wrong—not all of Starkad's gods had forsaken him. Starkad was on friendly terms with several members of his own pantheon. However, he wasn't big on worship these days. It was hard to put his faith in a higher power, once he'd realized they were as flawed as anyone.

Freya's back room was a stark contrast to the main shop. Stainless-steel racks for computer servers were built into the walls. An ajar door behind her hinted at an array of wires and blinking lights. It was her server farm. She'd kept up with technology and understood that most modern wars were fought digitally.

Starkad and Gwydion took seats in leather and metal chairs that surrounded a glass-topped table.

"Mead?" Freya offered.

"No, thank you." Starkad's refusal overlapped Gwydion's. No reason to unintentionally get caught up in some oath he wasn't prepared to fulfill, and sharing mead with a god frequently led to unfavorable contracts.

She smirked. "Fair enough." She reached into a cabinet and brought out a bottle of whiskey and three shot glasses. She set a glass in front of each of them, poured drinks, and settled into her chair. The fur cloak draping the high back gave it a throne-like appearance.

They knocked back the liquor, and Starkad let himself appreciate the burn of the smooth liquid sliding down his throat.

"What can I do for you?" Freya asked.

Starkad hoped this conversation went in the exact opposite direction of the one he expected. "There's a war you've been avoiding."

"I'm not the only one." She glanced at Gwydion.

Gwydion slid his empty shot glass across the table, from one hand to the other. "I can't ignore it anymore. Not now that she's involved."

Freya sank back into her throne, and her expression sagged. "I won't help my family kill each other."

"You can't sit this out forever." Starkad had had this argument with her countless times across the centuries. Today, it needed to go differently.

"Urd is a spinner of bullshit. Those prophecies were the musings of an intoxicated Fate. They're not a fucking roadmap. How many times do I have to tell you this? How long until you forget and ask again?" Freya's frustration was tangible, choking the air.

Starkad never forgot Freya's position. He simply didn't understand her sitting back and doing nothing, while the others gods killed to maintain their power.

"People are dying," Gwydion said. "Innocent people. Human beings, who have nothing to do with this."

"They're not dying in my name." Freya's icy retort was softened by exhaustion. Faith and sacrifice gave the gods their power. And blood sacrifices were the most potent for any god of war.

Starkad reached for a new perspective to this argument. Anything he hadn't said in the past. "You refuse to read the prophecies, because you believe all of us set our own paths. That life isn't predestined. TOM is using those texts to take that choice from others. I'm not asking you to enforce the prophecies. I'm only asking that you not stand by idly, while innocent people are destroyed."

"Don't do that," Freya said. "Interfering is interfering. If I stop them, I've taken a side."

Starkad clenched his fist and resisted the urge to slam it into the table. "I'm not asking you to pick up a sword. I want information. Nothing more."

"About?"

"Destroying Hel."

Freya rose and gathered the shot glasses and whiskey. She set the liquor in its cabinet, lingering with her back to them. She returned to the table, but didn't sit. "Is there anything else?" Fire filled her voice.

"By refusing to do this, you take their side by default." Starkad was grasping for any angle.

"Don't pull that bullshit with me, Berserker. You're always welcome here, but not for that reason." She cast a sweet look at Gwydion. "See you in another century?"

"I do hope we all survive that long," Gwydion said.

Starkad couldn't leave things this way. "Freya—"

"*Out*. You've worn out your welcome. I command you to leave my domain." Her voice shook the foundation.

There were no hugs or pleasantries exchanged, as Gwydion and Starkad headed for the exit. As they stepped into the hallway, Starkad's blood ran cold.

Loki was strolling toward them. He grinned and paused in front of Starkad. "It's been a long time. What, six years?" Loki's voice was too loud. Too friendly. "You left us without saying *goodbye*."

Starkad felt Gwydion's arm against his, muscles tense. Loki wasn't known for overt displays of power, but his subtleties could be just as destructive.

"I got bored," Starkad said.

"Right." Loki glanced past him, to Gwydion. "How's tricks?"

"Mostly harmless." Venom dripped from Gwydion's voice.

It might be entertaining, how poorly most trickster gods got along, if it weren't intimidating to be in the presence of.

Loki shrugged. "That's a shame. More fun for me, I suppose. What brings you home, Berserker?"

"Missed the homeland. Thought I'd see how different it looked now." This was an instance where Starkad would take banal small talk over most anything. The conversation was stuffed to the brim with bullshit, but no one was dying.

"What's your verdict?" Loki asked.

Starkad made a show of looking around. "It's nice. I like what time's done with the place."

Loki clucked. "You never struck me as the sentimental type. Speaking of— How's the girl?"

"Girl?" Starkad's tension skyrocketed. He refused to discuss Kirby with Loki. "Morgana? I hear she was destroyed. Or close enough." She had been a goddess who sided with TOM. Urd's prophecies predicted her downfall at the hands of a mortal woman and a god-turned-man, and they had been right.

Though, if she hadn't hunted the god and the woman he loved, would she have met her fate? In the end it didn't matter. Whether the prophecies were real or of the self-fulfilling variety, as long as TOM believed them, people would continue to die.

"Hmm... yeah. Shame about that. It's always sad to lose the nutty ones." Based on Loki's tone, it was anything but sad. "But I mean *the girl*. The sexy, barely-legal blonde you took from the campus under the pretense of her being dead. Your Valkyrie?"

Starkad forced his jaw to stay unclenched. He wouldn't react. He couldn't. "My what?"

"Are we still pretending she's nobody?" Loki looked between them. "In that case, the cadet you kidnapped. Does that ring any bells?"

"Nope. I left because there was really nothing substantial hiding in the wings at TOM. You're all as shallow and predictable as I thought, and I was tired of playing the game." None of that was true, but if they'd known who Kirby was from the start, Starkad had missed too much about their inner workings.

"My mistake. Hey, tell me something else, then. Next time we meet, what are the odds you'll try to kill me?" Loki asked.

"Fifty-fifty."

Loki extended his hand. When Starkad took it, Loki pulled him close. "You can pretend it's not her, but we know exactly who she is." Loki's stage whisper clawed over Starkad's skin. "Why do you think I brought her into TOM? In fact, I never lost track of her. The question is, can you get to her before Hel does?"

Loki let go and strode into Freya's shop without waiting for a reply.

Starkad was already reaching for his phone, pretenses be damned. He dialed Kirby's number, adrenaline spilling through him. There was no answer. "Call me back the instant you get this." He clipped off the words, disconnected, and called Min, to repeat the scenario.

"He could be lying." Gwydion didn't sound like he believed his own words.

"That is what he does."

Gwydion grimaced. "Unless the alternative is funnier."

And for Loki, mass murder was hilarious. *Fuck.*

CHAPTER FIVE

Kirby was on her feet, sprinting the short distance to the waiter, before her mind caught up. A knee to the back of his leg knocked him off balance. She twisted his wrist, and snagged the knife from mid-air as it fell from his hand.

He landed on his back. She pressed her knee to his chest and the blade to his throat. A steak knife would be a messy way to kill, but she'd do it if she had to.

"I'm sorry." He started to cry. "Did I get your order wrong?"

Disgust and doubt churned in Kirby. This was him. It had to be.

"*Kirby.*" Min's voice was sharp.

"Let me up, please." The waiter was sobbing now. "I'm so so sorry." He shook under her leg.

Was she wrong? No. She didn't read these things wrong.

A pair of strong arms wrapped around her, pinning her own arms to her sides, and Min lifted her off the waiter.

She struggled against the binding grip, but the best she could do was kick and thrash her head, and Min didn't flinch away from either.

"*Kirby,*" he barked again.

She paused long enough to look at the waiter. He stared back with wide, red-rimmed eyes, as he sat and scooted away from her on his ass.

Told you it was paranoia.

Kirby didn't want to believe it.

"I'm going to go." The waiter scrambled to his feet.

Min set Kirby down. "Wait." He caught the man at the door. "I'm sorry." He pulled out his wallet and extracted a wad of cash.

Kirby could grab the knife. She could cross the room and execute the waiter before Min could stop her. No hesitation.

He's just a waiter.

"Please forgive her." Min handed over the money. "She's going through a huge loss, and it's hit her hard. This stays between us?"

The waiter glanced over Min's shoulder at Kirby, fear oozing from him. "Crazy fucking cunt." He looked at Min again. "Between us. Yeah. But I'm telling management no more room service."

"That's fair." Min sighed, and locked the door behind the man when he was gone. He turned to Kirby. "Explain yourself."

Rage and self-loathing burned up her throat instead of an answer.

Min had been told, and he believed, that Kirby was a honed and trained killer. Starkad had also said she'd *struggled with a few things* when he pulled her from TOM.

Min didn't expect to deal with *unhinged.* He was more concerned than upset.

She stared him down, anger flashing cold in her eyes. "I didn't think this would be necessary, but apparently we need to lay down some ground rules."

"I beg your pardon?"

She stalked forward and jabbed a finger in his chest. "I'll kneel at your feet and suck your cock. I'll play your filthy baby-girl when we're fucking. But you do not *ever* get to undermine me when it comes to my safety. If you want to go carelessly about life, ignoring threats because they can't hurt *you*, I can't stop you, but don't jeopardize me in the process."

"You tackled a hotel employee and held a knife to his throat." Now Min was angry, but not about that. "And I don't want you to *play* at anything with me. You're here because you want to be. In this room and any time you're in my bed. If you're not happy with the arrangement, never do it simply because I asked it."

"Thanks for the lecture, Mr. God. Do your views on consent tie back to the fact that you've spent centuries looking for a dead woman because you had some good times while she was alive? I never asked for that."

He raised an eyebrow. "Now isn't the right time for this conversation. Not while we're angry."

"That's the perfect time for the conversation. Unless you'd like me to leave for good."

This wasn't about the waiter then. Kirby felt trapped with Min. Given the way she described the man from TOM, he understood her wariness. Now was the time to show her that she held all the cards in this relationship. He stepped aside and gestured to the door. "The clothes are yours to keep." He tossed his wallet on the table. "You can take whatever is in there. I don't want you here against your will."

"Why do you keep throwing your life away for her?" Kirby stayed rooted to the spot. "For a woman you've known less than a quarter of a century in total?"

Something she'd never asked before. They'd had similar conversations in her past lives, but never with so much venom. He was uncertain if the answer would make things better or worse. "I haven't always pursued you. I didn't meet you for the first time and think, *I'll surrender portions of my existence finding her again*. Neither did Gwydion." It took time. Knowing her across multiple lives. Her begging him to find her again, and him hating the idea of losing her until he did.

Hurt flickered across her face but vanished behind fury. "Good, then. I guess. No, I know. Good."

"Starkad always has, though. He's never lost faith in you." That should soften the blow, and maybe they could shift this conversation to something less defensive.

Kirby's falter lasted longer. "Yes he has."

"If you're staying, temporarily or otherwise, come sit down again." Min stepped past her, to the food cart. "Try the fruit. Unless you're concerned

TOM poisoned it." He wasn't poking fun at her. She obviously believed there was a threat, even if there wasn't one.

"TOM doesn't do poison. Too unreliable." She still didn't move.

Min filled two plates with fruit and brought them back to the living room. He set one on the coffee table in front of the couch, and settled back into his seat with the other.

"Whatever issues you and Starkad have—and no, he's never said such a thing—I guarantee his universe still revolves around you," Min said.

Kirby clenched her fists, and her chin quivered. Otherwise, she was stone. A stunningly fierce statue, in the middle of the room. Pygmalion would be smitten all over again.

Min continued. "When Gwydion first met you, when I did, you were another mortal woman. One with a tragic ending, but all mortals die. We'd witnessed it a thousand times each. Even the second time I found you, and after that, when Gwydion met the beautiful woman who reminded him of his past, it was a coincidence."

"In Rome." Her voice was quiet.

"Yes. He met Starkad a short while later, and learned who you were. Gwydion wished him luck in finding you, shared the news with me, and we went on with our existence. We're gods. We fuck, we move on. A mortal who dies and comes back is still a mortal."

Kirby sank to the ground on her knees, an ocean of emotion roaring across her features. Fear...

Hurt... Regret... Disappointment... "Then I remembered."

Min set his plate next to hers, his food untouched. "It all came back to you before you died. I knew by then that you were going to haunt my memories forever, regardless of what came next. When you begged me to swear that we'd find each other again, I agreed without hesitation. I promised you that and my heart."

"Her. You promised *her*."

Min wasn't going to argue the semantics. Kirby had the same soul and heart. The same name and appearance. Her experiences in this life had changed her, but that didn't erase the past. "It was similar for Gwydion. I'm certain Starkad never liked the arrangement, but..."

"I've— She's never remembered with him before." Kirby's gaze was haunted when she looked at Min. "You can't hold me to promises she made."

This part of the conversation never changed. That was almost a relief. "I don't. I never have. You and I always fall in love again. Yes, I know what you like, and I don't hold back when it comes to wooing you. But your decision to stay with me is always yours."

Min wanted to pick her up. Lift her from the ground and cuddle and console her. Instead, he grabbed the plates and sat across from her on the rug. He placed her food in front of her.

Kirby moved her knees from beneath her and sat her ass on the floor. "If I don't fall in love with you, what happens to you? Is this an *I mate for life* kind of thing?"

"You tell me *no*, and I move on. The offer I made you a few minutes ago was sincere." He popped a bite of honeydew in his mouth and let the flavor wash over his tongue. It didn't mask the bitter thought of losing Kirby.

"Just like that?" she asked.

There was no *just* about it. "I've given you my heart and soul and everything you've asked for, but only because we both wanted it. I won't stop loving you, but I also won't demand you do the same in return. I only ask that, if you do, it's without reservation."

"Kind of too bad Mark never learned that lesson." Kirby ate a grape. And then several more.

She was comparing him to a man she called a sociopath? "That man at the house? He didn't love you. You told me that yourself. You referred to him as obsessive. What you and I have is different."

She took her time with a piece of pineapple. "*I'm not obsessed with you,* says the god who's waited more than a thousand years for a dead woman."

"I need you to understand the difference." He was wounded that she would compare him to a stalker and killer. "Not just for me, but also for you. I look because I promised I would. Because you asked and I agreed. If you tell me to leave, or if you walk away, I'll respect that."

Kirby was silent, as she finished the rest of her fruit. "I'm not insane or paranoid. I knew that waiter, and he works for TOM."

"You made him cry."

64

"That's what we're—*they're* trained to do." She trailed her thumb over the scars on the inside of her wrist. Was she aware of the habit? "Seize every opportunity to use someone's prejudices and indoctrination against them. Crying? No one likes to deal with crying, especially men. If it looks like it will earn sympathy or discomfort, rather than hostility, it's an option. Racism? They spin that in their favor. If we were in public when that *waiter* felt threatened, he'd draw attention to you as a means of deflecting or escaping."

Min understood the tactics. He wished they weren't Kirby's default assumption. "Or he was simply terrified and didn't know how else to react."

"You had a part in the decision to leave me with TOM"—Kirby's tone shifted to cool and emotionless—"so I'd learn to survive. This is a part of that training. You can't be selective about which parts you deem useful, after choosing on my behalf to subject me to all of them."

"It doesn't work that way. I didn't sign off on the curriculum, and I didn't say my decision was without fault."

"This is a core component of protecting myself. That was the point, wasn't it? So I'd learn how to not die, and you could keep me longer?"

Keep me. He didn't like the disdain in her voice. "I explained—"

"I can walk away whenever I want. Now, anyway. I get it. I heard you." She kicked to her feet. "Did you trust them? These women you think are me? If they're me, then you could afford me the same courtesy. If you still refuse to respect my training, why the fuck am I here, and why the fuck did you subject me to it?"

Min heard her frustration. It echoed his own. *We don't hit people.* The condescending retort froze in his throat. He wasn't speaking to a child. Kirby was right; she'd been trained to spot danger. To see it lurking where no one else did, and to eliminate it before it was a threat to her. He couldn't fault her for that. Not only was it exactly what he'd hoped for, but the hints he'd seen of her skill and prowess were also beautiful. Terrifying. Haunting and awe inspiring.

He remained seated. If he stood, he'd tower over her. Given how much she interpreted in every gesture, there was no reason to add another implication to her irritation. "You're right," he said. "I did trust those past yous, and I did want you to learn these skills. If you see him as a threat, I believe you."

Her smile was strained. "No you don't."

"No. I don't. But I'm trying. It will take both of us some time to see things from each other's perspectives. I don't live my life looking over my shoulder constantly. I don't fear anything."

Except losing her permanently.

"This friend of yours... When are we supposed to meet him?" Kirby asked.

Min rose. He suspected the topic of her past would come up again, but they'd reached a middle ground, and that was acceptable. "Whenever you're ready. His shop is open during the day, but he's happy to meet with us after hours." A benefit of working with a brownie. Min would bring him a small gift—if it was too ostentatious, the man would be offended—and in return, Gareth would share his knowledge.

"After we move to a more modest room, something a TOM agent hasn't staked out right in front of us, I'm ready." Tension still had Kirby's body coiled tight, but the annoyance had faded from her voice.

"Why would we move?"

"Don't get me wrong. I love the pampering. I'm getting spoiled by the lifestyle. But he knows where we are, and a room at the Holiday Inn draws a lot less attention than the executive suite at The Ritz." She fixed him with a stare. "You want to see the world through my eyes. This is it. Safety is an illusion, every person is a potential threat, and *better safe than sorry* wins every time, even if it means a little humiliation."

He couldn't imagine every second of every day in that manner, but he was getting an inkling for her perspective. The waiter was hardly a threat, but if this would make Kirby happy, Min would comply. "I'll call Daz. He can make the change while we're out. Then no one knows it was us, checking into the new place."

"Thank you." Her smile was worth the concession.

He made his phone call, and they were on their way. The bookshop was less than a kilometer away, so they decided to walk.

Every person is a potential threat. Kirby's words echoed in his thoughts. He couldn't fathom it.

"Tell me what you're seeing right now," Min said. He was looking at London's beauty. The old buildings mixed with new. The crowds. The scents of car exhaust and threatening rain.

"Almost every person who can see us is staring. Most of them won't try to hide it. They want to know what a stunning, statuesque blonde is doing with a black man. They don't see your beauty. They sense your presence, but they misinterpret why it makes their pulse race."

Kirby slipped her hand into his. "And now several of them are looking away, either in embarrassment or anger. If we can't blend in, we have to stand out to the point where people actively try to ignore us." She drifted closer, until her arm brushed his. "And while they do that, I'm looking for the opposite. The individual who's so average, most people will never notice them."

"You never stop to simply enjoy the scenery." The realization saddened him.

"I can't afford to." She shook her head. "What?" She jerked her hand away and stopped in the middle of the sidewalk, looking around her, whipping her head in every direction so quickly it looked painful.

People grumbled but parted around her.

Was this a component of acting so awkwardly people wanted to ignore her? Not based on the panic splashed across her face. "Kirby?"

"I heard… Where's Gareth's shop? Specifically?"

Min gestured in the direction they'd been walking. "Two blocks that way, on the corner. Easy to spot."

"We need to go. Now." She was sprinting toward their destination before she finished speaking.

She maneuvered through the crowds like they were an obstacle course. Min couldn't navigate the throngs so easily.

He reached the shop a moment after watching her vanish inside. When he walked through the door, his heart stalled. Books were strewn everywhere, with displays and shelves toppled.

The damage looked superficial. Thankfully.

Min's gaze fell on Kirby, who stood at the front counter, and sadness rolled through him. Gareth was slumped over, dark-red blood spilling over his hands and already drying in the pool around him.

"Your friend?" Kirby asked softly.

"Yes."

"I'm sorry." She stared at the counter.

Min reached for her. "It's not your fault. We need to call the police."

"It is my fault." She nodded at a sheet of paper under Gareth's hand.

Min stepped closer, careful not to disturb anything. It was a page torn from a book, and it was facing away from Gareth. The handwriting in the margins was in English, but the original text wasn't. "What does it say?"

"It's about a maiden of death, who takes lives though she knows the price of losing…" Kirby fell silent. "The rest of the book is gone. We need to be too."

He'd like to wait. Tell law enforcement what they knew. He didn't need Kirby to tell him that was unwise.

Something beeped once, sharp and distinct. The floor under them rumbled.

"*Get down*," Kirby yelled.

Flame and debris exploded around them.

I won't lose her again.

CHAPTER SIX

Kirby had been in the middle of explaining her everyday reality, to Min when a man whispered in her ear, "You used to be a legend."

Her body seized, and she whirled to find the speaker. Even with his voice low, she recognized it as belonging to the waiter she'd attacked. The one who fled their room in tears.

She scanned the streets, searching for his face. There were too many people, none of them running or moving abruptly. He could be any of the blond men walking away from her. Any of the backs wearing a hat.

"Kirby?" Min's question interrupted her search.

Apparently the conversation about how he interacted with her while she was working wasn't over.

"I heard…" It didn't matter. The waiter was gone, and there was a reason besides her that he'd been here, or she'd have a hole in her somewhere. "Where's Gareth's shop? Specifically?"

"Two blocks that way, on the corner. Easy to spot."

Kirby was already running, weaving through the crowds, not looking to see if Min kept up. She charged inside the shop, and stalled a few meters back from the counter. A man was slumped over, a single sheet of paper pinned beneath him.

She tried to keep up a minimal conversation with Min, but her mind was racing along the situation. They were being set up. There was more to this than a dead shopkeeper, though she did mourn the man. He hadn't been a combatant. He hadn't done anything but seek knowledge, and there was no reason to kill someone for that.

This wasn't right. They needed to go.

The ground under her feet rolled, and the sound of an explosion ripped at her ears.

"*Kirby.*" Min's shout mingled with the noise, and he threw his body over hers.

She tucked herself beneath him and screwed her eyes shut, as the store rained down around them. She hated the practical part of her, arguing that he was less likely to take damage so this was okay. It made her feel cowardly and callous.

The noise was deafening but only lasted a few seconds. She felt fine, and not just because Min was an excellent shield. He hadn't covered all of her. Dirt and smoke should be caking her skin and clogging her throat.

She pried one eye open, and shock raced through her. Nothing was touching them. The debris seemed to hover millimeters above them. "Are you doing that?" She winced at the fear in her voice. How powerful was he? Was this why he kept himself away from combat? He wasn't just impervious, he could also repel threats?

He shifted, and their surroundings did as well, collapsing further but still not falling on them. She couldn't see his face from this position. Couldn't read his expression.

"No." The word was filled with awe and reverence. "You are."

"No. Nonononono."

"I've seen it before. You did it in Kuwait. You saved an entire building of civilians from a stray scud."

She couldn't... She wasn't...

Her memories insisted it was true.

"You can expand the shield," Min said. "Grow it slowly and use it to push the rubble away."

Rubble was tiny little bits. This was a stone building, on top of them. "I can't. I don't know how." She was helpless. She hated that feeling. Unless the rocks wanted to face her in hand-to-hand combat, she couldn't do anything.

Sirens bounced eerily around their temporary prison.

"If you do it now, we can be mostly clear before they get here."

Not in time to get away. Not that she was concerned with escaping. They'd play the victims and be on their way. *Play.* A building had fallen on them. They *were* victims, but Kirby hated being associated with that word.

That didn't give her the knowledge to do what Min suggested. Kirby didn't even understand how the shield was there. She couldn't feel it. She tried to grasp how she was doing it. To find the edges and push them out. Her mind met emptiness.

"Can you do it?" She tried to keep the panic from her question. "You covered me. You're strong enough to push up, aren't you?"

"Once your shield comes down, I'll be crushed, just not dead. I'm not impervious, but I heal impossibly fast."

She swallowed a string of curses, as frustration clawed at her throat in place of smoke. "If my shield wasn't there, you would have crushed me when the building did the same to you. What were you thinking?"

"That I couldn't lose you again."

A fist clenched around her chest. What was it about her that made him go to so much trouble, life after life?

The sound of voices and shouts drawing closer saved her from having to process his words. It was time to do something else she hated—pretend she was a damsel in distress.

"Help." It was too easy to let the fear flood her cry. "Anyone? We're here. Hello?"

Kirby and Min waited as patiently as was possible when buried alive, while rescue workers dug them out. Her shield fell without her permission, but what landed on Min was light by that point. The sun had moved halfway across the sky when they finally emerged.

The rescue team was amazed that, beyond being a little dusty, neither Min nor Kirby was hurt.

The police didn't talk to them for long. Min got as far as saying they were here for books and showing them his ID, and they were cleared to get checked out more in depth by emergency services.

Kirby couldn't imagine what that was like—getting out of sticky situations by tossing around a famous name. The idea of being so distinctly in the public eye made her skin crawl.

She and Min waited in the back of an ambulance, no longer important to the chaos, now that they'd been cleared. He was on the rear tailgate, keeping half an eye on her and half on the crowds. She sat on a stretcher. Where was their EMT? She itched to get out of here.

"I used to think we'd make an amazing team, if you weren't already spoken for." The hotel waiter's voice clawed down her spine. It mingled with memories of her life at TOM, sounding too much like Mark's and dragging up every time he'd threatened, terrified, and abused her. "But you'll never be what you once were."

He jabbed a needle into her upper arm. A wave of drowsiness swept over her.

The effects of the drug burned away just as quickly, as fire spilled through her veins. She whirled, to find him staring at her wide eyed.

Min wasn't stopping her this time. Determination filled her. This agent of TOM had killed an innocent man. He could have killed others. Casualties like that were meant to be avoided in war, not intentionally created.

"I've been in the history books for more than a thousand years." She didn't know where her words came from, but they rolled out on a threatening growl. "Your faith is based on my works. I'll be a legend for eternity."

"How are you not—" He cast his gaze about wildly and backed up.

Kirby grabbed his wrist. The electricity and flames boiling under her skin was unfamiliar, but right. And they were delicious. "You, on the other hand, will be forgotten after today. TOM won't remember you, and you most certainly aren't going to Valhalla."

She yanked him closer, despite his struggles and the fear spilling from him. She brushed a thumb over his cheek, and the life drained from him.

The strange feeling evaporated, leaving an empty pit in her gut and an ocean of confusion rolling inside. She screamed at the top of her lungs, forcing shrillness into the sound, and scooted away from the lifeless body.

An office appeared at the ambulance. "What the—" His hand fell to his club.

Kirby pointed. "He... He was starting his checkup... And he just... He fell over. I don't think he's breathing." The fake panic came easily, thanks to years of practice and a stressful day. Her nausea helped bolster it.

"Step aside." Another technician shoved past her.

She stared at the waiter's body—a guy whose name she couldn't even remember—as emergency services tried CPR.

It had been too easy to take his life. She was Kirby the Killer. Death was her training and her life.

But this wasn't the same, because she wasn't in control. She swore she heard Mark's voice, and that snapped something inside.

Ridiculous. You were protecting yourself. Protecting Min.

She was acting out of fear and delusion, not rationale. And if she didn't get that under control, she might make the wrong decision next time, just like she had with Mark.

Starkad didn't like waiting. He'd been doing it for more than a thousand years, yet he never mastered the concept. Sometimes life called for it, though.

Gwydion was making him look like a god of patience. "I'll go without you." He wanted to hop the next plane to London.

"You put everyone at risk, especially Kirby, if you do that. Our panic, acting irrationally and without a plan, is exactly what Loki hopes to incite."

Gwydion rolled his eyes and gathered his luggage. "Or he knows you'll refuse to act, and he's tormenting you."

They were in his hotel room and had been trying to reach Min and Kirby for more than an hour.

"I'm taking action, just not in the way you'd like. You know better than most that trying to out-think Loki is a path toward madness." Not because Loki was brilliant, but because trying to outwit him led to indecision, and that was death. Starkad grabbed the remote and flipped on the TV.

"You're going to watch movies? How the fuck are you not going out of your mind?" Gwydion demanded.

Starkad was ready to explode with frustration, but panic didn't solve problems any more than inaction did. "I'm checking the news. If TOM was in the same place as Kirby, odds are high someone died." *Please don't let it be her.*

Instinct said she was all right. He didn't have that nagging, ill sensation he'd experienced when she tried to kill herself. When Gwydion found her in the ally. Every other time she died.

But experience insisted something was wrong, and Loki's words taunted him.

"*Fuck.*"

Gwydion's curse drew Starkad's attention to the screen. The BBC headline read *Explosion in London*, and the anchor was discussing whether or not this was a terrorist attack. There wasn't a count of injuries or deaths yet.

"That's where they were going," Starkad said.

The explosion was meant to draw this kind of attention. To distract from something else. At least, if TOM was behind it. And this was definitely their MO.

Now Starkad was worried. "We need more information." He reached for his laptop. Fortunately, with Gwydion staying behind after Mark's death, he was able to gather their things and bring everything here.

"We have more fucking information. We *need* to go after her."

Starkad wanted to. The desire itched across every nerve ending. "In the amount of time it takes us to get there, the entire world can change. If we leave without more intel, we risk making things worse."

"So once again, you're going to sit on your ass while she suffers. You're going to put her in danger, because you think the outcome might be bad if you act." Accusation lined Gwydion's tone.

Starkad tensed, and anger surged inside. "If she was in the explosion, we won't help her by running out of here without a plan. Especially not knowing her status. If she wasn't badly hurt"— which instinct still said was true—"she knows how to handle herself."

"Don't you want to know if she's safe? Do you even care?"

Starkad's rage tore from him in a loud roar. He pinned Gwydion to the closest wall, by the throat. "Of course I fucking care," Starkad growled. "I don't know how you justify asking me that. I'd burn this world to the ground if I thought it would save her."

"So you keep saying. But she continues to die." Gwydion stared back with cold eyes. "We need to do something." A tremor ran though him, amplifying the fury in his retort. "I can't wait. I've done that for centuries."

Starkad held his gaze. The tension that flowed through the room was tangible. Anger hummed in Starkad's veins, amplified by concern. Gwydion wasn't a trained fighter, but he could grapple with the best of them when he felt inspired. And he was a powerful god when he summoned what

79

he had access to. Could Starkad beat him if it came down to it?

Gwydion's pocket chimed. Starkad let him go and grabbed his phone. *Min* flashed on the screen. Starkad put the call on speaker. "You're both safe?"

"Yes." The certainty in Min's tone was reassuring. "You know?"

"The bookstore made the news," Gwydion said.

"I lost my phone in the process." Kirby's voice came through clear and firm. "We had to deal with emergency services. Move hotels. We're clean, though."

Starkad could breathe again. "Good." He wanted to ask more, but they couldn't discuss details over open lines.

"I need to talk to you." Kirby's voice softened, and the hint of pleading cracked through him.

He ignored Gwydion's glare and took her off speaker. "Okay. I'm listening."

"He was a friend, from school." Her tone was tight. "He knew…"

"Kirby?"

"Everything." She gasped the word out.

Loki's words were back, taunting Starkad. But the rest of this conversation had to be as casual and coded as anything they discussed in public when they were on mission. "You know how people like to talk."

"I'd like to know more—" She bit off the words, and empty static filled the line. "About my family history. The woman I was named after."

She should have her memory back. What was he going to tell her? Then again, sifting through all those lifetimes had to be a mess, and it didn't mean all of the images in her mind made sense or hovered near the surface.

"How far back do you want to go? I can tell you some vivid stories from the old country." Were they fooling anyone who was listening in?

Loki or TOM? Not likely. A random law-enforcement agency that Loki might or might not have pointed in their direction? Most certainly.

Her laugh was strained. "I'd love to hear stories about the old country."

Starkad swore he heard a thread of fear in Kirby's request.

"We'll be in your part of the world in a couple of weeks. We should have coffee. Catch up," he said. Thankfully, it would only be another day or so. He wasn't waiting any longer to see her for himself, have a normal conversation, and ensure she was all right.

"Sounds great. I'll see you in a few weeks." Kirby continued the charade to the end.

"See you then. Be careful." Starkad disconnected and tossed the phone back to Gwydion.

Gwydion snagged the device out of the air, scowl in place. "Min was right. The passion you two have is enviable."

It really wasn't. Their passion set them on this path, and in the end, it was going to be what devoured and destroyed them. That didn't make Starkad feel it any less intensely.

CHAPTER SEVEN

Min couldn't erase the image of Kirby taking the TOM assassin's life from his mind. Death happened. He saw it every day, and she'd been trained to deliver it.

She was right. If they were going to make it through this, and if he wanted to be a part of her life, he had to give her the same trust he expected from her.

He didn't like that she'd killed, but he understood why. Doing so publicly felt reckless, but she was safe, and that was the most important element of the day.

They stepped into the hotel room Daz had secured for them. The entire place would fit in the living room of the suite they'd left behind.

Kirby latched the door behind them, draped her arms around Min's neck, and crushed her body and mouth against his.

Heat roared under his skin, amplified by the lust that spilled from her. Instead of affection, desperation was a tight core in the middle of her desire, muting the intensity.

That didn't stop him from kissing back. He lifted her so she could wrap her legs around his waist without breaking the tight lock of their lips, and carried her further into the room. He'd never required an emotional attachment from sex; it was purely a physical act. Except where she was involved.

He set her on the floor again, still embracing her. "Are you going to continue to use me for sex?" What he meant as a joke came out with a harsh edge.

Kirby raised an eyebrow and pressed her body closer. Her curves were sculpted and unyielding, like the woman herself. "How many times since we met have you chided me for saying something similar?"

"I don't use you."

"We can argue semantics, or we can fuck." She scraped her teeth over his chest, through the fabric of his shirt. Her hunger was to fill a void she didn't like having inside. The lost emptiness spilled from her, muting the passion flowing through the room.

None of that made him want her less. His body was alive with the need to take her. Then again, and again. "We can do both."

"Win me over. Show me why they all fell in love with you." Kirby let go of him and backed away.

Min wanted to argue that things didn't work that way, but that was exactly how love worked. Besides, this woman was fire and desire, and so much about her sang to his soul. And she'd just challenged him. "As you request."

He'd already dominated her. Enjoyable in the moment, but he wanted something else. He suspected she did too. With one arm under her legs and one at her back, her scooped her up, carried her into the bathroom, and set her on the tile.

It was a tiny closet of a room, with a ridiculously small tub, but it would do.

She reached for the first button on his shirt, and he grabbed her wrists. Her playful smirk sent need spilling inside. "No. Let me."

"Are you going to restrain me if I don't?" She was too tempting.

"I'll make you do this alone if you don't."

Kirby pouted. A deliberate, adorable expression.

He nipped her bottom lip. "I promise you'll enjoy this."

He stripped away her dusty, torn clothes a piece at a time, savoring the removal of each new layer. It was like unwrapping his favorite gift. And then she was naked, proud, and stunning, in front of him.

Min wasn't as deliberate with his own clothing. Not that he was reckless in its removal, but there wasn't much room in here for a drawn-out show.

They stepped into the tub, and he let the water from the shower sluice over them. He dragged a washcloth over Kirby's body, lingering and applying tantalizing hints of pressure to each erogenous zone. She whimpered and sighed and pressed into him when he massaged the terrycloth across her breasts. Her inner thighs. Her lower back and ass.

84

When he slipped between her legs, she gasped and ground against his hand. He only lingered long enough to clean, though pulling away from her heat was its own torture.

She planted her palms on his chest and glided down.

"No," Min warned.

"Or what?" Mischief sparkled in her eyes, and desire flushed her skin. She was calling his bluff.

He wasn't prepared to walk away, so something else had to give. With a twist of his finger, an invisible restraint bound her hands behind her back. Her light laugh implied she thought she'd won, and made his cock twitch.

Kirby's gaze drifted down and lingered.

Perhaps a different flavor of teasing was in order. He soaped his hands and stroked his erection, watching her watch him. Each pass was slow and deliberate, and he let the pleasure whisper through him. It wasn't the same as having her wrapped around him, tight and warm, but it was enough to make him groan.

He rinsed the soap from both of them. The act was an excuse to slide his bare hands along every inch of her skin one more time. Temptation and the buck of her hips begged him to slip a finger or two inside her. To stroke her silken pussy until she begged for release.

Soon.

Min turned off the water and released the restraints on her hands. He took his time drying both Kirby and himself, then led her back to the bed.

85

Kirby molded her naked form to his, lighting desire aflame everywhere skin met skin. She draped her arms around his neck and hovered her mouth over his. "How much did Starkad tell you about my leaving TOM?"

The abrupt question was jarring. "Not much. He said you'd been injured, but he got you out."

She shifted her body, and friction built between them. "He lied."

"Oh?"

"I've never been out." Her growling whisper rolled over him. "Part of me will be trapped there until either it burns to the ground or I do."

He mentally recoiled at her cold resignation. "No."

"You can't change that." She dropped one hand to wrap it around his shaft, and traced her thumb over the head. "Starkad can't. Gwydion can't. I can't. It is what it is."

Min didn't have a response. The combination of grief and pleasure wasn't one he cared for.

"But you can accept me for who I am," she said.

"I do." The reply came easily.

She let go of him and stepped back. The yellow light danced across her smooth flesh, highlighting her sculpted form. "No, you don't. But I hope you'll get there." She knelt on the bed, bowed her head, then looked up at him through her eyelashes. "Fuck me? Please?"

As it always had, the begging undid him. He pushed her shoulders, forcing her back onto the bed, and pinned her to the mattress. There were no magic bonds this time; his weight and attention would hold her in place.

He covered her in hungry, open-mouthed kisses, starting with her lips and moving to her jaw and neck.

She squirmed and dug her nails into his back when he lingered on her nipples, devouring one before moving to the other. The scent of her sex mingled with the desperation spilling from her and amplified his arousal.

When he kissed below her waist, reaching the core of her desire, she was already slick with anticipation. He dragged his tongue along her folds, lapping at her musky nectar. As his licking grew more intense, she gripped his short hair and ground into his face. It was so easily delightful to lose himself here, buried in her, in whatever way he could be.

He drew patterns on her clit, relishing her cries of orgasm. As she hit the first peak, he slipped two fingers inside her, drawing out the moment. He eased off to let the world settle around her—a few seconds, maybe more—then dove in for another taste.

Min pushed her to orgasm again and again, until her voice was a dry rasp and the tension had evaporated from it. Then he knelt between her legs and thrust his cock inside her.

She arched into the penetration and fisted the sheets in her hands. She was so beautiful. In pleasure. In pain.

Being inside her mended him. It was as if they became one like this.

He built to a rapid pace, slamming against her, focused on the physical rather than the lingering whisper that something was still missing between them.

Kirby wrapped her legs around his waist, feet on his ass, holding him inside. The buildup and ecstasy in the air hummed over his skin, drawing him toward orgasm. He grunted as he spilled inside her, feeling their auras mingle, and for a moment, their souls merge.

The world seemed to stop around them as he slid out of her, lay on the bed, and pulled her into him. There should be nothing but bliss in his mind and heart, but he couldn't ignore the empty pit. Was he going about things the wrong way with her?

Perhaps. This Kirby was impulsive and reckless. It wasn't about his accepting that she was a killer; she'd been born a Valkyrie, all those centuries ago—created specifically to live with death. However, she had scars she didn't want to acknowledge. If she wouldn't, he couldn't help.

They lay in silence, as the sun crept across the ceiling. In her past lives, it wasn't unusual for them to spend all day in bed, fucking and recovering. Here, her nervous energy was contagious, and it made his skin crawl.

"What did happen?" he finally asked. "Why did Starkad take you out of TOM when he did?"

Kirby's laugh was sharp. "Talk about a mood killer of a question."

"Is it?" There was no post-coital bliss lingering in this room. There was physical satisfaction, but the emotion behind it was all wrong.

"Things were brutal for me. For all their students." She rolled away from him, and the few inches between felt like an eternity of space. "Mark—Well, I've told you about him. Brit... She said she loved me, and then told the people in charge that I'd abused my power to force her to sleep with me."

Kirby trailed off.

Min propped himself up on one elbow, to look at her. She was staring at the inside of her wrists, tracing the scars she insisted were her fault and hers alone.

She met his gaze, expression blank. "I think Mark behind the entire thing. Brit says he was, though I don't know why I trust anything that comes out of her mouth. But when you tell me you've pursued me throughout history, that you've surrendered everything, I can't help but wonder, how is your obsession different from his?"

The question was like a slap, and Min stared back in disbelief. "I don't know how you can ask that. Do you feel the same about Starkad? Gwydion?"

"To a point." She turned her attention back to her wrists. "But they've never demanded I give them everything."

"Neither have I."

"But you have. You do. *I give you all of my love, now and for the rest of my existence*. That's oppressive. It's terrifying. I don't know what you'd call it, besides *obsession*."

Saying *it's love* wouldn't disprove her point, but Min had no other answer.

She shook her head. "Gwydion tried to move on. Starkad? He's been by my side for years in this life, and he's *never* demanded my affection." She trailed off with the last words, her voice so soft, Min barely heard.

"If he had—if six weeks ago he'd asked you to give him everything—would you?" Min was guessing, but the unrealized sexual tension between Kirby and Starkad was suffocating.

"Yes. Because I was obsessed too, and it wasn't healthy."

Min struggled for the right words to make her understand. "I don't ask anything of you that you're unwilling to give. That's always been the case."

"But it's still obsession. I need you to say that. I need to know you get it."

"I won't tell you that how I feel is anything like what Mark did to you."

She climbed from the bed and yanked on whatever clothes she grabbed first from her bag. "Right. Of course you won't."

CHAPTER EIGHT

It was always disorienting for Gwydion to come home. He managed to avoid Wales for decades at a time because of it. The forests he'd become sentient in were long thinner, replaced by homes and businesses and massive commerce centers.

He wasn't anti-progress. However, as he and Starkad stepped into a modern cafe, whispers of the power this place used to hold flitted across his skin. The birch and ash and oak that once grew here left their strength behind, to sing from the walls and the dirt.

Kirby and Min were waiting at the far end of the dining room. Recognition flickered in her eyes when she swept her gaze over them, before she continued her surveillance. Tension radiated from her casual posture.

"Does she ever relax?" Gwydion muttered.

"Typically not without a large dose of sedatives. Even then, the dreams haunt her." Starkad strode toward Kirby and Min.

Gwydion understood nightmares all too well. That didn't make it any better that Kirby dealt with something similar.

A sugary smile splashed across Kirby's face when they approached. The expression might as well have been painted on, but genuine happiness lingered underneath. "Hey, lover," she said sweetly.

"Missed you, kitten." Starkad kissed her on the cheek, before taking the seat next to her.

This was five-hundred flavors of revolting, the most distasteful part being how phony the exchange was. Gwydion ached to be closer to Kirby. To cast aside this bullshit act, forget about prophecies and past lives and everything that kept them apart, and spend months getting to know her. He still didn't understand how Starkad had stayed reserved and removed about their relationship for so many years.

Gwydion took a seat, not caring that he couldn't see the entrance, but careful not to block Kirby or Starkad's view.

"We can talk openly. Mostly. Keep the high-suspicion words to a minimum, and I'll keep us from drawing attention." Blending in was one of Gwydion's powers. It didn't work with Kirby or most TOMs, because they were always looking for things that were *too normal*. But for the standard person, who wanted to ignore the world and go on with their life, it was easy to project an aura of *there's nothing to see here*.

Kirby leaned in, her arm brushing Starkad's then resting against it. "Like what you did with those guys, last time I saw you," she said.

"Very similar to what I did with the police in Salt Lake." Gwydion added the details, to emphasize his lack of concern with being overheard.

Kirby raised her brows and pursed her lips. "So, you know what we were up to, given we made international news. What kind of fun were the two of you having?"

The truth stuck in Gwydion's throat. How was he supposed to dash her faith like that?

"We went to see Freya. To ask if she know how to destroy Hel. She told us to fuck off." Starkad obviously didn't have the same hesitation.

"Oh." A wave of emotion splashed across Kirby's face, bleeding from disappointment to disgust and back to neutrality. "Just like that?"

"More or less," Gwydion said. "We also ran into—"

"What happened in the bookstore?" Starkad talked over him.

Kirby rolled her eyes and looked past Gwydion.

The waitress set afternoon tea in front of them, complete with *bara brith* and cakes. He smiled at the familiar taste of home, and something told him Kirby was behind the order.

"Ran into whom? Since we're all being honest with each other these days. All the secrets are out. Everyone knows everything." Kirby said dryly, when the waitress was gone.

Starkad clenched his jaw. What was it about this one detail that he wanted to avoid sharing? "Loki."

"Oh." If Kirby was tense before, it was nothing compared to her rigid posture and stony expression now. She could have been carved from marble. A stunning piece by Michelangelo—*Valkyrie in the Cafe.*

"He knows who you are and where you were," Starkad said.

Kirby huffed out a sigh. "So how'd it go? Did the encounter end with his death?" Her words sounded as if they were chiseled from stone as well. Granite, perhaps. "I'm guessing it didn't, from your use of present tense. Why don't you know how to destroy Hel? Or Loki?" She looked at Min. "You're older than all of them, aren't you? You don't have any insight into their creation, and therefore, possibly, how to end it?"

Min shook his head. "Coming into existence isn't the same as watching someone else become and grow. We were all very much in our own parts of the world, until the Greeks, the Romans, and your people came along. By then, your gods already existed."

"They're not *my* gods. Even the original Kirby was cautious with her loyalty." She sank in her seat, grabbed some speckled bread, and nibbled listlessly.

Gwydion didn't care for the nervous energy that hummed in his veins. It had been there since the lights went out in the safe house. He expected it to ease up when they were all together again. When he saw Kirby was safe. Min, even. However, the situation felt less secure than ever. He wanted to get through this. To have answers and a resolution, and to move on with life.

He knocked back his tea in a long gulp and waved the waitress over for more. Why hadn't their group met up at a pub? The alcohol wouldn't get him drunk, but the taste was comforting. "Did you discover anything besides sensational explosions?"

"Death." The word dropped heavily from Min's lips.

Kirby scowled and grabbed a cake. "I saw a page with Gareth. The book was gone, but they left that page for me to find."

"Can you give me a few sentences?" Starkad grabbed his phone. He typed as Kirby recited a line, then turned the screen toward her.

Her eyes grew wide. "That's it. If you have a digital copy, why did we need to talk to Gareth?" She swiped the screen, to expand the image.

"His copy had his notes," Min said.

"This is about us." Kirby's voice was soft, as she nudged the phone back toward Starkad. "About you, teaching me. This is about us at TOM. We never read this quintet in school."

"Are you surprised?" Gwydion didn't try to hide his sarcasm. "Are there passages in there about you being in London, as well? About you looking for this book? It doesn't map out the entirety of existence. It's a few vague suggestions that are easily misinterpreted. How did Loki know where you were, and how do we prevent him from finding you again?"

"*Us*," Kirby said. "How do we prevent him from finding *us* again. And it doesn't work that way."

Starkad set his phone on the table but didn't let go. "She's right. We do our best to stay hidden, but we can only make decisions based on the information we have. We stick to the plan, unless there's evidence that data has changed."

Which was a great excuse for sitting on their asses, like they had in Norway.

"The instant you start trying to guess what the other person is thinking, you lose yourself in indecision. You never move forward." Kirby picked up Starkad's thought without hesitation. "Can I get a copy of that book?"

Starkad jabbed his phone screen several times. "You've never been interested before."

"Because it's really dry reading, and I didn't realize the versions at home were different from school. I want to know what they didn't teach us, and I promise not to consume it all in a single night." She almost smiled.

Because they understood each other. The last few years with Kirby had impacted Starkad as much as it had her. Something about him was different that hadn't budged for centuries. And it reflected back on her. It didn't change the fact that her time with TOM caused her so much harm, but seeing even a glimpse of joy poke through was incredible.

They moved the conversation back to Starkad's hotel room, and for the first time in days, something felt right in Kirby's world.

She was still adjusting to being involved in the decision-making side of missions. She liked it. She appreciated that Starkad always had her back when she said something. Then again, he always had.

During her hearing with TOM. Saving her after. Taking her thoughts and instincts seriously on mission. His concern when she called after the bombing, and the way he'd accepted everything she said, rather than questioning whether or not her past had come back to haunt her.

She'd never realized how much respect he showed her, until she had butted up against Min's questioning everything in London.

It was nice to be heard, even if the discussion was largely the men throwing out names of supernaturals they knew, and then nixing them as potential sources of information.

"What about Aeval?" Min asked.

"Who?" Another name Kirby didn't know. Then again, she didn't to know them all. Most of that information wasn't important to a group of people trained to only focus on and kill specific gods, the way she had been with TOM.

Starkad furrowed his brow in that deep-concentration way she used to swoon at the sight of. "She's queen of the fae."

"There are fae?" Kirby didn't know how she felt about that.

"There are," Starkad said. "I don't know her personally." He looked at Gwydion. "I didn't think you two were on speaking terms."

Interesting. "Ex-girlfriend?" Kirby asked.

Gwydion chuckled. "I keep thinking I can move on from you—she was one of those attempts—but you keep sucking me back in. Hoping to do the same to you."

"Pretty sure you did that once already." She hoped he would pick up on the innuendo.

Gwydion's smirk was the perfect confirmation. "Nice one." To Starkad, he said, "Aeval will see me. Especially if Kirby joins me."

Starkad's arm tensed where it rested against hers. "That sounds dangerous."

"I promise you it's not. It's hard to explain, but it won't be an issue." Gwydion looked Kirby over.

The appreciation and faint amusement in his gaze lifted some of the shadows lingering around her. "I never thought I'd get to meet a fairy."

"You will have to leave the weapons behind," Gwydion said, "but you don't need them anymore."

"So we've seen." Min's mutter was soft, but the hard edge sliced through Kirby.

She ignored him. "They make me feel safer."

"No iron." It was one of the few times she'd heard a *no arguments* tone from Gwydion.

Most other metals didn't exactly make for great weapons. "No iron." She'd make the concession. If he trusted this woman, Kirby supposed she could go without. Not that she liked having to do so. This whole *you trust them so I will* thing was spreading thin.

The four of them wrapped up what was a flimsy plan at best—go visit Aeval and take things from there—and Gwydion and Min stood.

Starkad slid Kirby a room key. She shouldn't have expected anything different from any other mission, but the sight cut through her worse than normal.

"You sleep in separate rooms?" Gwydion sounded surprised.

"And the two of you don't. Do you have a point?" Starkad's tone and expression gave away nothing.

Gwydion shook his head. "No. See you both in the morning. Unless you'd like to join us?" He focused on Kirby.

She could. Her body heated to scorching at the idea of another night with them. So where did her hesitation come from?

All of the people she fucked thought she was someone else. She never used her real name or gave them any pertinent information. But Min and Gwydion saw her for her, and still thought she should be someone else. Her most recent encounter with Min proved that. He still wanted *his* Kirby in his bed, not her.

"Actually, I need to talk to you." Starkad's request saved her from having to make the decision.

She swore the tension in the room thickened like instant pudding, but she was grateful for the reprieve.

"No worries." Gwydion waved a casual hand, but his tone defied the words. "We'll catch up in the morning."

Kirby settled back in her seat. This was familiar—Starkad's hotel room, the unrealized sexual tension, the completed mission planning, the key she didn't want to pick up. But it was filtered through a lens that distorted it.

She twirled the rectangle of plastic on the table, and watched it spin.

"You can stay here, if you'd like," Starkad said. "It's not a command or an assumption. It's an option. "

A bitter laugh bubbled in her throat, and she choked off most of it. "No. We're not doing that. Don't be like them. Don't change who we are just because I've got a few new memories."

"I'm not." He sank in his seat—the casual posture she was used to seeing at home. "This isn't a matter of *share my bed; I'll finally give you what you want*. I don't expect you to magically be the woman who gave me immortality. I don't want that. If you'd like some company, with no expectations, stay."

But that was the problem. He never had expectations, and she always did. This switch that had flipped with him was different from Min or Gwydion's, but it was just as bad. "Don't. Don't treat me differently than before. Nothing has changed."

"You're right. And at the same time, everything has. I don't have to keep secrets anymore."

Kirby's harsh chuckle escaped this time. "And that's the problem—that you still think you had to before."

"See this from my perspective. Trade places for me for a moment. If it were you, looking for me—if you'd lived through the centuries, knowing I'd died a dozen times, and then you found me as a young man—would you have told me everything up front?"

"Yes." Her certainty was only external. Would she really have done things much differently than he did? She had no idea what he'd been through over time, but when she thought Brit had killed him, Kirby wanted her to suffer for eternity.

"You wanted to know about you in your first life," Starkad said.

So he had understood her flimsily coded plea over the phone. It was nice to know the double talk hadn't changed between them. "There was a man in London, behind the bombing... I recognized him from school. He was younger. I don't remember his name." She still felt a twinge of ambivalence about that. Why did it matter? "He's dead now."

Starkad didn't flinch. Because of course he didn't; he was responsible for her being a part of this lifestyle. This was what he'd wanted for her. "What happened?"

Kirby related the incident in the hotel—her recognizing the TOM, and Min's letting him go. Irritation flashed across Starkad's face, and she felt a smidge of vindication. She went into detail about passing the TOM agent on the street, then finding the shop owner dead.

When she reached the explosion, her brain stalled. It was a struggle to wrap her thoughts around summoning shield against the rubble. That she'd done it instinctively. That moment wasn't what she needed answers about, anyway.

"We were in an ambulance, because emergency services showed up and insisted on checking us out, and he—the TOM—was masquerading as an EMT. This power flowed through me. Words that weren't mine. Arrogant. Vengeful." The memory left a bad taste in her mouth.

Starkad raised an eyebrow. "Which part of that wasn't you?"

"Funny." But she felt a little better at the trace of humor in his question. "It was like someone else—this original her—was speaking instead of me, about how he didn't deserve to go someplace like Valhalla. It didn't feel like anything I'd say. And then I touched him, and he was dead. The power that I had to do that... I've never felt anything like that before." What bothered her about it?

Where the hell was that instinct when Mark was standing behind her, with a gun pressed into her back? Why did it come naturally for her to direct this new power at an almost stranger, but not at the man who tortured her for the majority of her teenage years?

Min thought she'd acted irrationally, but he didn't get it. Hesitation, not eliminating obvious enemies, had cost her too much. Starkad understood that.

None of this internal exchange made her feel any more in control of her reactions at the scene.

"Technically, you're not allowed to take a life as a Valkyrie if you don't send the warrior to Valhalla." Starkad's light tone cut through her self-doubt.

She forced a smile. For all the concerns she had about the situation, pissing off the gods didn't even make her Top Ten list. "Or what? I'll anger Odin? Freya?"

"She won't like it."

Part of Kirby winced away from the reality of his statement, but she was grateful for the chance to

ALLYSON LINDT

take a tangent. She could redirect her angst to something she didn't have control over. "Did she really tell you *no?*"

"She also told me you still pray to her."

Kirby should have known better. "Not after this." Admitting it hurt. She was tired of having her trust and faith ripped to shreds.

"I'm sorry." Starkad sounded genuine.

At least the mistake of following Freya had all been Kirby's. It wasn't as though promises were made and broken. "The gods disappoint, right? That's why we don't have an issue, defying their arbitrary commands?"

"True."

"So this thing I did—taking his life, saying that stuff…" Kirby didn't want to drift back on topic, but her brain wouldn't let it go. She needed a reason for her inconsistent actions.

"Sounds a lot like you, back then."

Wonderful. She was making irrational decisions because she had dead people living in her head. "You didn't say *her*."

"There are things about you that are different. You're still your own person, but you have their memories, and it's all your soul." Starkad lightly slapped his palm on the table in a steady pattern as he spoke. He was struggling with parts of this as much as she was.

And that was comforting. "None of the others were like she was then. Or like I am now."

He shook his head. "You grew more reserved as the centuries passed. As *civilization* hid its desire for destruction under language and learning and art. And you were raised differently in each life."

"At least I was frequently the fantasy girl for someone to win and own." Her amusement was laced with sarcasm.

Starkad raised his brows in question.

Her smile was genuine this time. The bleak humor in the situation gave her a twisted kind of satisfaction. "Farmer's daughter, lady in waiting, artist's muse, preacher's daughter, general's daughter..."

"Highly trained assassin for vengeful gods," Starkad supplied.

That hadn't made her list. "Whose fantasy is that?"

"Mine. Except that I'm not looking to own you."

She believed that. He'd made a lot of decisions on her behalf that she didn't agree with, though she understood why more each day. But when she wasn't hurting herself, he trusted her opinion and respected her choices.

He never would have questioned her actions in The Ritz, the way Min did.

Starkad sighed and flexed his fingers. A tell he never let show in public. He was as restrained and composed as she was if anyone else was looking. "I've never been through what you go through when your memories come back," he said. "I can tell you whom I knew back then, and whom I know now. I can tell you that you're more like you were in your first life than I've ever seen or heard about in the time in between. And I can tell you that I always fall for the parts that never change."

"Like what?" This was something else she struggled with. Starkad, Min, and Gwydion spoke about these other women she used to be like irresistible forces with a magical energy that drew them in and made them fall. Kirby didn't buy it. "You keep talking about how you always love me. How there's always a similar thread. I don't see it in them or me. I don't even know who I am. How do you?"

"You're always compassionate until someone proves they don't deserve it." He reached across the table and covered her hand. The simple gesture blanketed the roaring chaos in her head. "Always intelligent. Fierce. Defending those who can't defend themselves."

"You speak quite highly of these dead women." A hint of bitterness slipped into her voice.

Starkad stroked a thumb along her knuckles. "I speak that highly of you. I haven't been blind for the last decade."

A fist clenched around Kirby's heart at the genuine affection in his voice. She didn't want to feel that now. Not after everything that had transpired between them. "I knew you were watching," she teased.

"I've told you that."

"But I like hearing you admit it." She couldn't hide behind the playfulness the way she wanted. The world and revelations of the last week weighed too heavily on her. "Thank you. For the information. For helping me try to pursue Hel and

Loki." She pushed past the desire to stay here all night, and forced herself to stand. "I should get back to my room."

He stood, but didn't turn away before she saw the splash of regret. "All right. One more thing before you go." Starkad strode to his bags, dug to the bottom, and extracted a leather sheath. He returned and handed her the dagger.

A familiar shock spilled through her when she brushed her fingers over the worn leather. She knew what she'd see before she slid the blade free. The light in the room seemed to vanish into the onyx blade. The dagger had been hers in her first life. The first thing about her past that felt like it belonged to her, and not to someone else.

The bone hilt fit her hand perfectly. She stepped back from the table and made a few tentative swipes. "You still have it." Why did the words lodge in her throat with emotion?

"I promised you I'd keep it safe."

"But... why now?" She'd never seen it in any of her other lives. Not that she'd had many with Starkad.

He closed the distance between them again and rested his mouth near her ear. "Because this time, you're coming back to me."

A shiver of heat blanketed her. Kirby pulled back to meet his gaze. What she saw staring back from crystal-blue eyes was too complex to put into words, but it made her heart soar and die at the same time.

Starkad pressed his lips to her forehead and muttered something in a language few spoke anymore.

She still recognized the, *Be safe, my love.*

"You too," Kirby whispered and strode from the room. It was the hardest time she'd ever had, walking away from Starkad, even though she was only going next door and it was the right thing to do.

CHAPTER NINE

Kirby struggled under Mark's weight. Her limbs felt coated with concrete with each punch she tried to throw, or kick she tried to execute. Terror clawed at her senses, and she couldn't grasp the training that said she had this. She was supposed to be better than this, and she was failing.

"We all could have been happy together." There was too much joy in his voice as he ripped off her top. "But you were never anyone. A name with no history to back it up. Your entire legacy is a lie." He was the room-service waiter now.

Defiance pushed a retort to the tip of her tongue. An argument, that she didn't even know his name. She wasn't the one who would fade from the history books. That had already been proven.

The protest froze in her throat. She wasn't those other women. The original Valkyrie was a different person.

Pain seared through her body when he sliced a blade across her throat. Not the good kind of pain.

There was no rush of endorphins here—only the gurgle of blood, bringing agony.

"Hmm… you're healing." He was Mark again. "That means I can play with my toy all night." He dug the knife under her ribs.

A whole new world of pain shredded through her, and a scream tore from her throat. Kirby didn't want him to see her breaking, but she couldn't hold back the terror and suffering.

Each jagged slice her felt like a portion of her body was being clawed away, and then healing again.

"We've always known who and what you are." Loki's voice filled the room around them, but she couldn't see him. "We gave you to him, and you broke. What a disappointment."

Rage joined her terror, and Kirby grabbed for everything she had. She was a fucking Valkyrie. Mark would suffer, and this time it would be at her hand.

Nothing happened, except the sound of three men's laughs filling the room.

Kirby's eyes flew open, and her heart skidded into her ribcage over and over. Whispers of the dream lingered with pain in every spot Mark had cut into.

Above it all, she heard the *snick* of a latch, and the hotel-room door closed, cutting off the light from the hallway.

Her room at the Waldorf Astoria, in New York, swam into view around her. At least Brit wasn't in this dream, but it was a shame killing Mark hadn't banished him from the paralyzing taunts from her subconscious.

The odd thought rattled in her head. She didn't know a *Mark* or a *Brit*. She climbed from her bed, navigating the darkness with ease, and grabbed her dressing gown. She tugged the silk on over her nightgown.

The set was a gift from Gwydion. She'd never worn silk before she met him. Even if she'd had the money, the fabric had become nearly impossible to get when the imports from Japan dried up.

Gwydion had gone up to the roof, like he did so many nights. She'd never followed him before, but tonight she needed to see him.

Dim bulbs lit the hallway, and the richly woven carpet caressed the bare soles of her feet. They were on the top floor, so it didn't take much to climb the stairs to the roof.

Darkness greeted her as she stepped outside. The stars were so far away, and the lights of the city so far below. Gwydion stood at the edge of the building, staring down.

Kirby was glad she'd found him in this life. He was patient with her processing her past lives, he was fun, and he was incredible in bed.

He was also haunted. She saw it when he thought she wasn't looking—the distant stare and the shadows that hung in his gaze. As a Red Cross nurse, she'd seen that look dozens of times with her patients. She could clean and bandage wounds, but chasing away their torment was outside her training.

"You can join me if you'd like." Gwydion's voice was soft, and he never looked in her direction. "I promise I won't let you fall if you don't want to."

Odd qualifier. She approached with hesitation, her heart hammering in fear again. She gripped his hand tight.

"Look over the edge. I've got you." He didn't tug her closer.

She crept up to the ledge, forcing her limbs to move despite the terror that wanted to lock them in place. When she stepped up next to Gwydion, he wrapped an arm around her waist. The city was so far down. The smattering of cars, with their long hoods, tear-shaped wheel wells, and canvas tops, looked like toys.

"Are you all right up here?" He asked, his grip tight on her hip.

If by *all right* he meant *scared out of her wits*. But she trusted him to keep her safe. "I'm good."

Silence swept in around them, as most of New York slept. She leaned into him, resting her head against his chest, and staring out at the world. Could they stay like this forever? If they never left this rooftop, would she stay alive this time?

"It's tempting, isn't it?" Gwydion's voice sounded distant.

To stay here forever? Had he read her mind? "What is?"

"To take a step forward. To see what it's like to fly."

No. The vehement denial slammed into its opposite in her chest, and bile rose in her throat. She'd never wanted to end her life, but she had. She'd fantasized about it off and on, for years.

Kirby swallowed a whimper at the conflicting thoughts of life and death.

"I used to wonder—if I fell far enough, would it be enough to finally kill me?" Gwydion sounded as lost as she was.

She banished the foreign element of her mind that understood the sentiment behind his words. "Do you think about dying a lot?"

"Depends on your definition of *a lot*. Now that you have your wings, would you like to fly with me?" He extended his hand.

No, she screamed in her own head. That other bit of her pushed forward, tangling her fingers with his. Fear surged inside, but it was wrapped in calmness and anticipation. Two halves of her argued.

When Gwydion stepped forward, so did Kirby. It was simple—one foot off the edge, and let gravity do the rest. They tumbled down, into a pit of blackness with no bottom. Falling. Spinning. Never hitting ground.

Kirby jolted awake again. The light from the hallway spilled in under the door, and the TV droned on with some syndicated supernatural bullshit. Was she awake this time? No one was in the room with her. This was the tiny little room in London she'd fallen asleep in. The dagger sat on her nightstand, the faint light in the room bleeding into the soft leather sheath.

Knowing she was awake didn't push away the lingering traces of overlapping dreams. Go figure that the nightmares weren't gone. She refused to let Mark's ghost haunt her, but she had no idea how to convince her subconscious of that decision.

She climbed out of bed, fighting with the hazy dreams, clawing to put them in a box and lock them away.

Clothes. She needed those and air. She yanked on jeans and a T-shirt—the uniform of indoctrinated TOMs around the world—and grabbed the dagger and her room key.

The falling sensation rushed around her as she stepped into the hallway. The air, blowing past her face and whipping her hair out behind her. The second dream had been a memory, but it didn't end that way in real life.

She couldn't remember how things had gone instead, but in the dream she'd so desperately wanted Gwydion's words to be true. Hoped that, if she fell far enough, she'd hit the ground and not get up.

Kirby made her way to the stairs. Her room was on the fourth floor, with only two more floors above, and the staircase was an easy climb.

She wasn't surprised to find the door to the roof locked. She couldn't pick locks. Was she super strong now? Enough to force it open? Nothing in her past said that was an option, but the past hers were kind of pussies. She wrenched the handle, expecting it to give way.

It refused to budge past a wiggle.

She had to get out there. *Why*? Because sanity was on the other side of that door. Her dream-memory was wrong to hate the fear. If that was what waited for her, it was another flavor she'd never tasted.

She was the reason they'd survived the explosion in London. She'd done something similar in Kuwait. Kirby turned her focus inward and grasped for a shield she'd only summoned by mistake so far.

A warm glow sped through her veins and encased her body in an invisible bubble. She didn't see it when she opened her eyes, but she felt it. She twisted the handle on the door again, and this time it gave.

When she got back to her room, she'd call the front desk and tell them it was broken. Wouldn't do to have just anyone wandering out here.

There was no one else here, which made sense, given the trouble she'd had gaining access, but disappointment flitted inside at not finding Gwydion waiting.

Compulsion guided her feet to the edge of the building, where she sat, one foot dangling over the side. This was nothing like the roof of the Waldorf Astoria in 1942. A dozen electrical fans whirred behind her, choking the air with their noise. The street was near enough below that she could make out license plates on the cars.

If she fell, it would hurt like fuck—probably break a few bones—but it wouldn't kill her. The drop wasn't far enough.

She slid the onyx blade from its sheath. The city below provided enough light to bounce off the blade and fall into the shadows of the runes carved on the hilt. She didn't need to read the text, to know it said *Ill is it to leave the right undone.*

The words clenched around her chest in a way she didn't care for. They tied her to a past she didn't want to admit was hers. But the longer she stewed in the memories, the harder it was to ignore how much she felt in each one. Physically and emotionally.

She dragged the tip of the knife across her palm. Pain seared through her at the number of nerves she hit, and blood welled up from a cut that healed the instant it was created.

This agony was hers. It was tied to a past she recognized—one she'd had a say in, whether or not her decisions had been the right ones.

Kirby made another slice that vanished as quickly as the discomfort, leaving a streak of dark red as the only reminder she'd been injured. It'd be nice if the wounds inside healed as easily.

The door creaked behind her, and all of her senses cranked to full alert.

"Thanks for taking care of the lock for me." Gwydion's teasing comment calmed her again. The impulse to jump into his embrace snaked through her, the way it had for both him and Starkad when they walked into the diner. She wanted to wrap her arms around his neck and her legs around his waist, and kiss him until her lips ached.

That's what any past her would have done by this point in their relationship. And she was going to have to admit those lives were hers. That didn't change how she felt now, so she stayed put. "I was a little surprised you didn't get to it first."

"The view up here isn't as great as in New York, and to be honest, it kind of breaks my heart." He joined her on the ledge but kept his back to the city and his feet on the roof.

"I'm sorry."

"Nothing to do for it. But I'd rather see this place thriving and alive with new energy, the way it is now, than it be a pile of rubble."

She slid the dagger back in its home and set it on the rooftop by his feet. "Would you rather witness the changes or not survive to see them?" She would never dare have a conversation like this with Starkad. He was kind and sympathetic and wanted her to heal, but she felt his frustration and disappointment. She hated to be the cause of that. Gwydion would understand.

"You mean what we talked about in New York, all those years ago. I don't have the death wish I used to. I want peace, but I want to find it in this world." Gwydion glanced sideways at her.

"Me too." Her voice cracked, lacking conviction.

He settled a hand on her planted bare foot. Warmth and comfort seeped into her skin. "You don't have to pretend with me," he said. "If you don't feel the same way, I won't judge. I'm here for whatever you need."

Tears pricked her eyelids. Hearing him confirm he understood her darker thoughts lodged like a lump in her throat. She swallowed back the relief and confusion. "I don't know what I'm doing." The confession slipped out. Did she feel that way?

Yeah.

"I lit into Starkad for taking my choices, but I don't know how to make my own decisions. My entire life, I've let the current carry me. When TOM stripped my world from me—" Kirby needed to stop. She didn't talk about this with anyone. Even Starkad didn't get to hear her musings about the night he'd saved her. But the words wouldn't be held back. "I didn't know at the time I was trying to kill myself, but when I thought I was dying, there was so much relief. No one could tell me what to do anymore, but I wouldn't have to figure it out, either." She choked on a sob and almost held back the wave of emotion rushing through her. "I'm such a fucking coward."

"No." Gwydion managed to pour force, understanding, and sympathy into a single syllable. "You're a billion things, but *coward* isn't one of them."

"Maybe not in my past lives, but now…"

"Especially now." He squeezed her hand. "It doesn't matter that we don't know each other. I've been where you are. Not for the same reasons, and there's a part of me that argues mine weren't nearly as good as yours are. I'm not telling you to stop feeling that way, but I am saying, whatever it is you feel—good or bad or angry or happy or anything on the spectrum—I'll sit through it with you."

She couldn't talk about this. If she slid into a pit of darkness, it would take too much to climb out. That wasn't an option on mission. It was barely an option when she was home alone, having no idea why Starkad had jetted off to some new place without her. "Can I fly? Am I capable? I have wings," she said.

Gwydion raised an eyebrow and stood. He took her hand and pulled her to her feet. "We did in New York."

The rest of the memory flitted back into her head, carried on gusts and updrafts and freedom.

Back then, they had stepped from the ledge together, but they didn't plummet in an uncontrolled spin. She'd soared, with her hand clutched tightly in his. New York City, Staten Island, and the Atlantic Ocean had stretched out beneath them. It was dark and inky and stunning. And then they'd come back to the hotel, breathless and laughing. Filled with joy.

Kirby'd never been that happy in this life. The realization gnawed a hole in her heart. Flying wouldn't give her that feeling, but she could use a little freedom right now. "I want to try again."

"Okay." Gwydion tugged her to the center of the roof. "I'm not jumping off ledges with you, though. At least until you have a little lift."

Another snippet of memory tickled her mind. "But you can fly too." She hadn't been holding him up in New York.

"I can, but it's never the same for me alone. And Min's private jet is far more comfortable for transatlantic trips." He didn't have wings. Flight was just one of his gifts.

Her giggle felt foreign but good. "Let's do this."

She didn't have to reach as deep, to figure out how the flying worked. The knowledge was on the surface, summoning her wings and lifting her into the sky. Gwydion floated up to join her, and tangled his fingers with hers.

Kirby cut a straight line into the sky, the wind tearing at her clothes and biting her cheeks. When they were high above everything, including the tallest building, she glanced at Gwydion.

He nodded. She wasn't sure what it was in response to, but she let inspiration propel her.

They hovered in the air together, looking out over the city and the channel. Then she pointed herself at the ground and dove.

This was the sensation from her dream, but there was no fear here. Kirby was in control. She understood how far and fast she could go. She pulled up short before the rooftop, and they touched down lightly on the dusty concrete.

This was incredible. Her heart still soared above them. She threw her arms around Gwydion's neck and crushed her mouth to his.

He gripped her hips hard and returned the kiss, his desire swirling with her happiness. The hammering of her heart against her ribs was powered by something other than terror or doubt. This was incredible.

She pulled away with a gasp and met his gaze. A hint of reality slithered in, stealing her smile.

"What are you thinking?" he asked softly.

If she answered honestly, she'd ruin the moment. But the truth was jagged inside, insisting she let it out. "I've been going hard since the mission in London, and the one before that. If I slow down, like I did tonight, I'm going to slide. I can't do that."

"You can." He slid his hands to the small of her back, holding her close. "If that's what happens, that's what happens."

"No." That was so impractical. Her depression and self-loathing were liabilities.

He brushed his lips over hers. "Yes. You push through the darkness when it occurs. I'll hold you, if you want. Or I'll sit in the other room and slide chocolate under your door, if you'd prefer. And you come out the other side."

Kirby wanted to be comforted by his words. A little spark inside pleaded for her to believe him. But he didn't understand. She was reckless and had a death wish, and her actions were going to demand a price she was unwilling to pay.

CHAPTER TEN

Gwydion hated parting ways with Kirby and sending her back to her room alone, but after the highs and lows—literal and emotional—it was for the best. Not that he would have turned her down if she asked him to stay, but he wouldn't be the one to propose it tonight.

The next morning, her smile was too bright and her voice too chipper when she answered her door. She'd talk when and if she was ready. He hated being pushed into soul-bearing, and would resist the urge to do that to her.

"May I treat you to breakfast, m'lady?" He offered his arm.

Her smile loosened, and she hooked her hand around his elbow. "I'd love that."

Aeval was going to love meeting her. Especially with Kirby looking a bit like a modern fae herself, in a gauzy blouse and loose, flowing skirt. The clothing had to be a gift from Min, but it was deceptive. A long slit was hidden among the folds on Kirby's right side, and Gwydion guessed she had the knife she'd been playing with last night strapped there.

As with most things in Bangor, it was a short stroll to the coffee shop. They moved away from the hotel and the modernization fell away rapidly, giving way to older buildings that hummed with more of the magic that made Gwydion's blood sing.

"I remember this place." Kirby's voice wove into the underlying symphony.

"I didn't know you'd been here."

"Not here, specifically. And not now. Before. When you and I met the first time. The air feels the same." She sounded distant but calm. "When more than just a handful of fucked-up kids knew the old gods were real. When the god who commanded the trees told me I was the most stunning creature he'd ever met."

He remembered that too. It sparkled brightly in the sludge that was his past. "You were. You are."

Her laugh was light. "And yet, you've said that to so many women since."

"Only a handful, and it was what they wanted to hear." Gwydion wouldn't hide any part of his history from her.

Kirby slipped her hand into his. "How do I know you're not just saying it to me?"

"Because it's not what you want to hear."

"That's true." Her ego was attached to something other than appearance. She'd been raised to know she was beautiful and that it was one of her greatest weapons. "My memories told me I had *A List* in my last life."

He smiled at the call to the past. Each time they had sex someplace new, she would say it had always been a fantasy—sex with a doctor, sex with an entire battalion sleeping in the next tent, sex in the dressing room at Macey's—and that she was checking it off her list. "I'm not sure if you ever actually did, or if you were making things up as we went along."

"I'm not telling. But I had an impressive list after about six months with you," she said playfully.

They'd been stationed in Kuwait together. She was clergy, and he was a doctor. It was how they met. They were far enough from the front lines they never saw much action, and as the conflict wore down, they spent a lot of time getting to know each other. "Do you have *a list* now?" he asked.

"No. What does a girl like me put on a list like that?"

Fair question. "Sex in your own bed, without worrying about the consequences. Missionary position, I'm guessing."

"You could help me tick that box?"

"I'll tick as many of your boxes as you let me. Again. And again."

Her laugh was as magical as the currents that ran through this part of town. "What about going to the movies without constantly looking over my shoulder? A moonlit walk on the beach without wishing I had something more powerful than a dagger strapped to my thigh? Would you give me those?"

"Would that I could." Gwydion squeezed her hand.

They turned down a street walled by old buildings, with barely enough room for a two-lane street and the sidewalks that ran in front of shop fronts.

Kirby nodded at a Bentley, parked halfway on the sidewalk. "Check out the jackass."

"He'll get his." When it came to karma, Aeval and her kin were swift and direct in its delivery.

Kirby snorted. "Right."

Stepping inside the coffee shop was like passing through a gateway to whimsy. Light curtains fluttered in a breeze that didn't exist. Splashes of color and flowers covered the walls, and the furniture was tastefully eclectic.

"What is this revolting shit?" The harsh question came from a man at the counter. He wore a suit that probably cost more than all of the decor in the place combined, and held a paper coffee cup and a scone. "This is supposed to be the best fucking coffee in Wales, and you serve me shit-flavored water instead?"

Kirby started to pull her hand away, and Gwydion gripped tighter.

"I'm sorry you're unhappy, sir. I can make you a new drink." The man behind the counter matched the rest of the room and looked to be in his early twenties. He was probably ten times that.

The businessman knocked over the tip jar, and coins flew everywhere. "I don't have time for this bullshit." He tossed his drink on the counter, splattering the tile with coffee.

Kirby tugged harder, and a growl accompanied the glare she threw at Gwydion.

This was a painful sight. He understood her impulse to step in and make things right, but in the end, it wouldn't be as much fun. He leaned in, to rest his lips near her ear. "As much as I'd love to watch you take that guy down a notch or even just kick him in the nuts, they've got this. Trust me."

"One of these days, your *trust me* is going to wear out its welcome," Kirby murmured. "And behind you."

The man's phone rang as he stalked from the shop. His shout of anger could be heard through the door, after it shut behind him.

"Gwydion. It's been ages." Aeval's sweet, accented voice came from behind.

He spun, to find her watching them. "I try not to keep track," he said.

She cupped his face in her palms and pressed her lips to his. As kisses went, it was pleasant. She'd never sent the heat searing through him that Kirby did, but for a while, he and Aeval had been happy to distract each other.

Aeval broke away and twisted her mouth into disappointment. "Is this her?" She knew exactly where Gwydion's heart belonged and why he'd ended their romance.

"Yes."

Aeval looked at Kirby, then nodded out the front window. "Watch."

Kirby looked over her shoulder. Asshole-in-a-Suit was in his Bentley, gesturing angrily.

"I can't believe he's that pissed over bad coffee," Kirby said.

"My coffee is the best you'll ever have." Indignation lined Aeval's reply. "And he's not. He's furious because the largest share of his portfolio plummeted in price five minutes ago, and even though he saw it coming, he forgot to confirm the transaction when he went to sell this morning."

In Gwydion's experience, that was only the beginning of the man's bad news. It was never a good idea to insult the fae.

A large truck turned the corner at the far end of the street, its top swaying from the too-fast speed. A scooter moved into sight from the other direction. The moped driver tried to swerve, but there wasn't enough room. The truck veered to its left. The only place for it to go was into the Bentley. The crunch of metal screeched through the air, as the car was pinned between the truck and the brick.

Kirby gasped.

"No one's hurt." Aeval sounded casual. "But no one out there is innocent. We believe in making our own justice."

"Neat trick." Kirby turned back to face her, and Gwydion did the same. "Don't suppose you can teach me how to do it?"

Aeval dragged her gaze over Kirby, lingering on her face. "No, beautiful. The justice you deliver would clash with mine."

Kirby frowned. "Oh."

"Do you have a few minutes for an old friend?" Gwydion asked.

"For you, always." Aeval nodded to a table in the back corner. "Jayden, three large specials."

Gwydion pulled out a chair for Kirby, and scooted it in as she sat. He was home. He had this amazing woman by his side.

Too bad the serenity and perfection were flimsier than any illusion he'd ever cast.

Kirby was still making up her mind about Aeval, but so far, she was cautiously entertained and optimistic. And the coffee was incredible. She couldn't identify individual flavors, but it was like joy mixed with melancholy.

"Well?" Aeval nodded at Kirby's cup.

"It's really good."

Aeval was smug. "Of course it is. What can I do for you, handsome? Or did you just come by to introduce your Valkyrie? Not that I'm minding."

Gwydion's posture had relaxed since they stepped inside the shop. "She's not mine."

"Yet," Aeval said.

Kirby wanted to protest, but her tension was fading as each moment passed. Was it the drink? She didn't feel less alert or aware. She did a quick once-over of the street outside, ticking off all the available hiding spots for danger, and comparing it to the list she'd made in her head when they approached.

Nope. She was still seeing and processing it all. She just wasn't concerned about the consequences.

Really incredible coffee. And something she couldn't afford to drink ever again. Not that she could leave this cup half full. No reason to insult their charming hostess.

Aeval hid a smile behind her cup.

"I'm hoping you can point us in a direction." Gwydion sounded less stressed as well. "Toward someone who knows about Hel and Loki."

Aeval's cheer slipped, but flitted back in a flash. "You know the rule. We're not involved in their war. The prophecies don't mention fae. We never registered on Urd's radar until her people came here."

Irritation surged in Kirby but was squelched by something harsh. Not a fan of the drink after all. "A shift in power like that applies to everyone. It doesn't matter that the gods interact more quietly with humans than in the past. They still influence the world, and if some are intentionally destroying others, that influence is disrupted." Hel. Loki. Others like them. These gods were killing and torturing and brainwashing for their own gain.

"Some people and some gods will die, and others will rise, and tomorrow the world will still spin on its axis." Aeval fixed her with a hard stare.

"Hmm…" Gwydion didn't look affected by the tension or news, one way or the other. "You have that in common with Freya. She said something quite similar."

Kirby clenched her jaw at the reminder that her chosen deity had willingly refused to take part in such an important war. It couldn't be true. They misunderstood Freya, or something else interfered.

Aeval growled. "Freya is a coward. Her people created this mess—"

"Take it back." Kirby half rose in her seat, indignation pumping through her veins.

Aeval didn't flinch. "Save your worship for those who deserve it, Valkyrie. Like him." She nodded at Gwydion.

Gwydion covered Kirby's hand.

The unspoken message was louder than any words. *Stand down.* Kirby's irritation burned away the lingering effects of the coffee. She didn't care for being dismissed or leashed. A sliver of reason reminded her this was the place for diplomacy, and she argued back that Gwydion should have come alone in that case.

"You don't actually believe the consequences of this conflict won't reach you," Gwydion said. "That the outcome doesn't matter. You live in this world, rather than existing on the fringes. It's as much a part of you as you are of it."

"This is a truth." Aeval sighed and set her drink down. "You don't have to convince me. Our new leaders—the council, the representatives—they've turned us into a bureaucracy, and it makes me ill. I'm the fucking queen, and I refuse to let those assholes destroy everything. Besides, new gods would mix up life and add a new sparkle to the world. Nothing wrong with a little death and rebirth, as long as everyone has a fair chance."

Kirby's irritation faded. Maybe Aeval wasn't so bad after all.

"Point me in a direction," Gwydion said. "Tell me who to talk to. More than humans walk through your doors. You've heard volumes of gossip over the years, and you're brilliant at remembering it."

"It's true. I am." Was Aeval preening? "I want a kiss from your lover first."

Gwydion raised an eyebrow. "That's not mine to offer."

"Favor for a favor."

Kirby stifled a chuckle. This was probably the point where she was supposed to huff and be offended. To say her physical affection wasn't a prize to be traded on a whim.

Cliché request, but Kirby wasn't going to turn it down. It was a fucking kiss, and the stunningly manic queen of the fae was asking for it. "You're expecting me to balk."

For the first time since they arrived, Aeval looked like she'd been caught off guard.

Kirby half rose in her seat, leaned across the table, and brushed her mouth over Aeval's, before deepening the kiss. She lingered, pouring all her passion into the contact and mixing in a smattering of tiny nibbles and licks along Aeval's lips.

She knew it was a good kiss, and Aeval's and Gwydion's groans backed her up.

Kirby sank back into her seat, trying and failing to hide her bubbling giddiness under a shy mask.

Aeval brushed her fingers over her bottom lip. "That's worth a lot of information. Which is good, because what I know is big. The *Genii Cucullati* can give you want you need."

"The Hooded Spirits?" Kirby's past lives were supplying her with all sorts of ancient languages.

Aeval shook her head, amusement splayed on her face. "You speak in ancient tongues. You're full of surprises."

Knowing the words didn't mean Kirby understood their relevance

"Don't suppose you can get us into one of their *gatherings*," Gwydion said.

"Rumor is they're not fond of Min, if you still travel with him."

"Then he won't join me. I have a far more stunning date, anyway." Gwydion nodded toward Kirby. "And they owe me a favor, but not one I want to waste, gaining entrance."

Aeval pulled her phone, seemingly from nowhere. "I know a girl who knows a guy who can get you in for Summer Solstice."

Only a few days away. Convenient. Then again, the entire offer felt too easy. "What's it going to cost us?"

"We'll call it even. That was one hell of a kiss." Aeval licked her lips.

Kirby didn't buy that. "Is that the only reason you're offering all of this information and help?"

"Not the *only* reason, but pretending I'm that flighty is good for my reputation. I don't want you as an enemy, and I like this world and the people in it. Don't let your gods destroy life for the rest of us."

If only stopping the gods was as easy as something like going to a Solstice party.

CHAPTER ELEVEN

Min didn't like the way things were unfolding. Agreeing to let Kirby pursue this vengeance was a bad idea. What happened in London, with TOM pursuing her, reinforced the foolishness of it all.

He was trying to understand where she was coming from, but he didn't see it.

"This is going to destroy her." He paced his painfully small hotel-room, venting his frustrations at Daz.

The other god listened patiently, as he always did. "She may want that."

Another thing that bothered Min. Kirby not only didn't seem to fear death, it also was as if she pursued her own. A dangerous proclivity, to begin with, but far worse for someone who had died so many times. "I don't know what to say to her, to make her listen."

"You may not be able to say anything." Daz had been by Min's side for a few centuries. He'd witnessed Kirby come and go. He said he stayed because he owed Min, for saving his life. In truth, it was because Daz loved him. The passion that flowed from Daz was impossible to ignore. Min had made his feelings for Kirby, and his intent to continue pursuing her, clear.

Daz understood. That didn't stop him from trying to steer Min away from Kirby's memory, disguising the attempts as comfort, each time she died. "This may be your chance for closure," Daz said. "An opportunity to sever ties with her while she's still here, and not be beholden to a spirit you can never appease."

"I made her a promise, and it's in place until she decides she doesn't want it." Min had never considered Daz's suggestion before. So why did the words linger in his head today? "She's still the same beautiful, kind, brilliant soul I fall in love with each time I meet her." The difference was she now held a lot of beliefs he didn't agree with. "Even if she does have a taste for death."

"She's a Valkyrie. Starkad was, is, and always will be right about that. She was created to be a creature of war, and to take life when appropriate."

That wasn't where Min's reservations lay. "Sending a fallen warrior to the afterlife is different from executing a man on the street."

Daz nodded. "To you and me. To her, the streets are modern warzones."

"That's not true." But it was. Min had seen her as they strolled through Piccadilly Square. And again in the café here. She was always on alert. Always waiting for the next battle.

Could he accept Kirby if that never changed? If she continued to be this urban warrior? Was he capable of meeting her halfway when it came to her perspective of what a threat was?

Min didn't know.

As Gwydion strolled back to the hotel with Kirby, he bounced options in his head about how to break the news. In any other life, she'd jump at a chance like this. Now, he had no idea how she'd react. He didn't suspect she'd have a problem with the orgy side of things, but she might with the naked-without-weapons and surrounded-by-gods aspects.

"Are we going shopping, or will they let me in the door like this?" Kirby gestured to her clothing. "It sounds like a pretty casual event. Am I right?"

No and yes. This was as good a segue as any. "If you show up like that, they'll cut the clothes off you before they let you in."

"Nice." She cut her laugh short, and her footsteps faltered. "You're serious."

"I am."

"Are we talking no clothing at all? As in, we wear trench coats with nothing underneath, and check them upon arrival?" Her voice didn't give anything away around how she felt.

Gwydion knew exactly how this next bit was going to sound. "More like hooded cloaks and masks, with nothing underneath." That wasn't as true these days; clothing was optional, and masks weren't.

"Secret sex party? How very *Ninth Gate, Eyes Wide Shut.*"

Yup. That was what he thought. He tried to look offended. "The *Genii Cucullati* are older that most of us, and by *us*, I mean the gods. Their teachings have been lost, misinterpreted, and twisted, but as gods, they're still good, kind, and giving."

"And have solstice orgies."

"Which are not mutually exclusive from *good, kind,* or *giving.*"

"Touché." Kirby's laugh was back.

"Are you up for this, pet?"

"What makes you think I'm going to be your pet anywhere, let alone at some public and lewd display of lust?"

"Instinct. Wishful thinking. That night in Salt Lake."

She let out an exaggerated sigh. "Convince me."

He could do that. "You'll look completely harmless, and no one will have any idea you're one of the deadliest people in the room. And I'll buy you a collar."

"You say the sexiest things." Kirby tangled her fingers with his and leaned into him as they walked.

That went well. Now to convince Starkad and Min this was their best lead to keep moving forward. Not that Gwydion would take *no* for an answer from anyone except Kirby, but things would go more smoothly if everyone agreed.

"I'm not on board with this." Starkad trusted Kirby in any combat situation. He had no doubt that, with a weapon in her hand, she'd survive any urban warzone. He didn't like any bit of this, though. Not that he was willing to admit it was because of the envy, clawing inside. He didn't care about the sex. Or perhaps only a little. It was about how easily Kirby slid into things with Gwydion. Again. The one thing that never changed. "We all have other sources."

"Which we've tapped. These are our last resorts," Gwydion said. "We're lucky Aeval had anything. How many misses have we had before now?"

Dozens. Hundreds. Starkad had lost count.

The four of them were in his hotel room, discussing Gwydion's lead. Min was disconcertingly quiet. In the past, Starkad had gotten information from Brit, coordinated through Min with Followers of Urd for a safe house and relocation for the target, and planned the execution with Kirby.

Starkad didn't care for this decision-by-committee bullshit. "I'm opposed, regardless."

"You've had years together, playing the nineteen-fifties television version of *house*. Let Kirby choose to enjoy someone else's company for a while." Gwydion was never going to drop this.

Starkad looked to Min for backup and tried to ignore that Kirby hadn't offered any protest. "Do you think this is a good idea?"

"I'd go myself, if I thought they'd allow me in the door." Min shrugged. "These are peaceful gatherings. My only objection is they're going for reasons other than to enjoy the sex. If the goal is to meet the hosts, these two simply have to draw the right kind of attention."

The *drawing attention* bit was the other issue Starkad had with the idea.

"I doubt they're going to balk if I have two dates." Kirby finally spoke up. "Or is that some sort of orgy etiquette I'm not familiar with? Do I need to learn rules that don't apply at normal dinner parties before I go?"

"You already know the one that matters— consent is everything," Min said.

Gwydion lounged, very much embodying the cat who swallowed the canary. "A lot of the gods don't care for Starkad. Something about never knowing where he stands."

A huge drawback to centuries of fighting for whichever side would have him, before becoming a double agent in a war almost everyone felt strongly about. Even if that feeling was *leave me out of it.*

Kirby pouted. Over his not joining in? "So I have to leave my guns and my spotter behind?" she asked.

Ah. "You don't need weapons."

"I feel safer with them."

"Wear the earpiece. We'll stay in communication." Starkad was willingly going to spend the night listening to her date with Gwydion. But memories of the little gasps and moans she made when she was turned on danced in to distract him. They would make for a nice soundtrack.

"Earpiece it is," Kirby agreed. "If I can't go in armed, I feel better having you listening in."

He couldn't ignore the self-satisfaction that he was her bit of security.

"Be cautious." Min didn't look happy about this, despite not offering much protest. "Wounds from gods and other immortals are different than if the average guy on the street pulls a knife on you."

"How likely is it people will have any idea who I am, or care?" Kirby's flippant tone was marred with concern. She was taking this more seriously than she wanted to let on. "How likely is it I'll run into Hel or Loki there?"

On the thin end of slim, or Starkad wouldn't be agreeing to this regardless of the arguments. "Hel's not much of a sex-party person. Neither is Loki." He was too manipulative to be comfortable in a setting like that. He didn't have enough control in front of such a big audience.

"Unless it's funny," Gwydion said.

Not reassuring. "But you'll be on your guard."

Kirby nodded. "Always."

That should be reassuring. Kirby on mission was professional, precise, and perfect. But when it came to Gwydion and sex… The last week showed that her outlook changed. And Gwydion wasn't cautious. He was Kirby's flavor of self-destructive, sprinkled with cayenne.

Starkad had to trust Kirby. She was the best at what she did.

And in the meantime, he'd ignore the jealousy that she was doing this without him and hadn't put up a fuss about her escort for the evening.

Kirby hadn't expected the scene to literally look like it came out of a movie. Their car carried them up a winding driveway lined with lights, to a massive stone home. Hedges hid the building from the road. Not that it mattered.

She'd memorized everything about this place, despite not needing to for the plan. She didn't like going in without control, and committing the layout to memory let her pretend she had a little. The building sat on ten acres of heavily forested land, the closest neighbor was a mile away, and the main road wasn't much closer.

Daz had offered to act as their driver, but Gwydion insisted this kind of affair wasn't meant for uninvited guests, even if they waited outside.

When Gwydion pulled the Jaguar up to the front entrance, two men in masks, bow ties, and thongs were waiting to open their doors. One took Kirby's hand and helped her from the car, and the other took the keys from Gwydion.

Kirby paused at the base of the steps leading up to the entrance, and grasped her training as tightly as she could—stay alert, focused, and ready to act in a heartbeat. This was about to go from surreal and almost funny to very real and terrifying.

Gwydion offered his arm, she hooked her hand around his elbow, and he covered her fingers. "You ready for this?" he asked.

She nodded, and they climbed the stairs. As they walked through the double front doors, she held her breath, exhaling when they stepped foot in the marble foyer. The house was warded to only let people who had been invited pass inside.

Inside was more grandiose than the exterior. Some people wore cloaks. Gwydion had explained they'd remove them when the mood struck. Others discarded their cloaks at the door entered nude.

Then there were those like Gwydion and Kirby, who chose to dress for the affair. Though calling what she was wearing *clothing* was generously deceptive.

He was in mostly black, from the button-down shirt to his slacks, tie, and shoes. His corset vest was the only splash of color—black with red embroidery. The entire look was topped off with a black mask that had feathered wings.

She'd almost drooled when she first saw him, and hadn't wanted to take her eyes off him since. He also carried her only physical weapon. His sleeves were rolled up almost to the elbow—yummy times two—and he wore her dagger strapped to the inside of one. He could claim it was for play, it was difficult for anyone else to get to, and Kirby knew how to access it quickly.

They strolled through the foyer, where a handful of guests were in various stages of fondling and fucking each other. The casual, shameless display flooded Kirby with heat. This had just become very real.

She and Gwydion drew stares and whispers, as they crossed a floor lit with crystal chandeliers. Kirby was his opposite in her white—heels, thigh-highs and garter, panties, and corset. All of the fabric was lace or sheer and left nothing to the imagination.

Exposing her heart or mind to anyone was a nauseating thought, but this was exhilarating. The glances of appreciation, the adoring stares and murmurs—they were more intoxicating than watching the groups in the lobby.

She watched it all through a white feathered mask. The finishing touch on her entire ensemble was a gift from Gwydion. The white leather bracers were completely impractical for combat, but they hid her scars and were less restrictive than a collar. Kirby shouldn't have reveled in Starkad's scowl when he saw them, but she did. They were the equal and opposite of a gift her gave her years ago, that she'd returned since.

Despite all of that, Kirby was terrified to be here. Fear was supposed to be delicious. To flit on her tongue and amplify the desire that pulsed under her skin. It shouldn't matter where it came from, even if it was a side-effect of how many gods were here that could probably kill her in a heartbeat if they had an issue with her or her associates.

The souring in her gut must be because this wasn't just sex, it was also a mission. Mixing business with pleasure was screwing with her. *Carefree* didn't mix with *constantly on alert*. Not that anyone would see her trepidation. Her emotional mask matched the one covering the upper part of her face.

Gwydion bowed his head and placed his mouth near the ear that didn't hold a microphone. "If you squeeze my arm any harder, do you think you'll get juice from it?"

She hadn't hidden as much as she thought. She relaxed her grip and tried to breathe out her tension.

"What's the worst that could happen?" he whispered, as he guided her toward the edge of the room. Here people watched from the shadows, their attention focused on those bold enough to step into the light.

She raised her eyebrows in response to his question.

"Well?" he said.

Kirby had to put the gnawing discomfort into words. "We die. Everyone here dies. The city is consumed in a massive fireball of god rage." Saying it aloud made the fear less potent. She expected a reprimand from Starkad, or a growl. He was quiet. Good.

"Now be plausible," Gwydion murmured.

She had been, but she understood his point. *I die.* The answer stuck in her throat. That never bothered her before, and it didn't now. Did it? Her stomach squished with the question, and she shoved the reaction aside. "Nothing we can't handle."

"You're not leaving this life without me."

It both chilled and comforted her that he knew what she was thinking. "No, I'm not."

"That's my girl."

She shouldn't let such a simple, possessive comment warm her from the inside out, but it did.

"If you two are done, on the clock." There was Starkad's familiar growl, in her ear.

She suppressed an eyeroll. So much for seeking a little comfort. "I'll be a good girl. I promise." She meant the words for both of them.

"Not too good, I hope." Gwydion's comment overlapped Starkad's, "At least until this is over."

142

Was she more irritated with him, for assuming otherwise, or that she'd gotten to a point where he had to? It was tempting to throw all caution to the wind and go for broke while they were here.

And give him a reason to not trust you?

Kirby was tired of her every action having to be proof of her right to exist. With TOM, with Starkad, and now Min. She wanted to be her for her sake.

This isn't about proving yourself; it's about reliability. You need that from him, and he from you.

Reliability? Starkad had kept so many secrets. Shattered her faith in him into a million pieces. If he couldn't accept Kirby for herself—

By for *yourself, do you mean* self-destructive and immature?

She didn't like this version of berating herself. It hurt in whole new ways. She was capable of making her own decisions and choosing what wouldn't get her hurt.

This from a woman who revels in pain.

That was her decision too. She needed to stop arguing with herself, before it drove her insane.

Too late.

CHAPTER TWELVE

Kirby managed to quiet her inner war by focusing on the party. Not just the open and shameless displays of sex—though those were among the most brilliant things she'd ever seen—but the attendees themselves. Most were humanoid, but so many were exotic. Some with rainbow colors of hair and unique hues of skin. Others with tails, ears, horns, and hooves.

She knew creatures of all flavors existed, but she'd never witnessed any beyond those the gods at TOM kept as pets. Actual domesticated animals, not like the woman with the pink, sparkling mane and unicorn horn, who looked blissfully happy to be in a cage while dicks were shoved in her face.

The entire affair was incredible. Solo sex, group sex, submission, sweetness, and pain. The variety overloaded her imagination and made her pulse race. But she was most focused on those people on small stages, in the center of the room.

She wanted to be up there, with Gwydion taking her while the other guests looked on. She and he were supposed to attract the attention of the Hooded Spirits, but drawing the eye of everyone in the room was probably a bad idea.

Gwydion nodded at the woman in the cage. "A unicorn shifter. She's happy in there, and everyone else is safer."

"Safer?" First fae and now unicorns. Anything was possible in a world where an array of gods walked among mortals.

"She tends to lose control during sex. Rumor is it's the best orgasm you'll ever have, but the price for penetration is mutilated genitalia or, if she's too enraptured, death."

There went any illusions Kirby had about innocent creatures frolicking in the woods. There was a certain amount of respect for the unicorn, though. "If you're going to come and go, make sure it's big."

Hesitation crept in as the words slipped out. Would Gwydion think the joke was tasteless? Min had a problem with the way she viewed the loss of life.

"As long as you actually do *go*." Gwydion didn't flinch. "I'm not sure I'd give up my dick for a night of sex. Even the best sex I've ever had. Maybe I'd surrender a finger." His tone was serious consideration mixed with a hint of humor.

More of her tension drained away. "I need my fingers. For pulling a trigger. Picking my nose. Masturbating. Could I give up an earlobe, maybe?"

"I'd rather you didn't." He caught one of her lobes between his teeth and tugged. "Yours are cute and bitable. And it's not much of a sacrifice if you give up something you don't need."

Fair point. "So we're talking what would I surrender for the best sex ever? It can't be anything I use for work. Life goes on, even after an earth-shattering orgasm."

He cupped her face and dragged a thumb over her cheek. "That means no disfiguring. Marring your stunning-good looks is straight out."

"That's true." She let out an exaggerated sigh. This was fun. Dark. Twisted. Definitely fucked up. And he didn't have an issue with any of it.

"But... best sex ever," Gwydion said.

"How do you quantify that? You and I have had some pretty hot sex. And technically, I died after." Was that going too far? The dark humor worked for her, but she could almost hear Min's disappointment in her head.

Gwydion screwed his face up. "Good point. I can't say I've ever had better. Wait. Are you saying my dick killed you?"

"Not every time." She shouldn't be joking about this. The bits of her from past lives were horrified she found this amusing. But making light of her death was freeing.

As was Gwydion, not backing down from the teasing. The corners of his mouth were curled up. "Does that mean my performance wasn't up to par every time, if you only suffered dick-death sometimes?"

"I wouldn't say that. It was pretty incredible this most recent time. Though that thing with the latex in Kuwait..." She let the pleasant memories of sex on an exam table flit through her mind. "But if we're talking *The Best*, I think you'd know. The sky would open up, choirs of angels would sing…"

"And you wouldn't give up a pinkie for that?"

Kirby shook her head. "I'm not going to hobble myself for the ultimate orgasm. I'll take death." This time she was certain she heard a growl in her other ear. Starkad didn't appreciate this.

"What if there was a guarantee you could do it again?" Gwydion asked.

It didn't change her answer. "One—*The Best* sets an impossibly high bar, and all sex that isn't *The Best* feels like losing you virginity in the backseat of a Volkswagen, to someone with no experience. And two—even the best gets stale if there's no basis for comparison."

"Valid points." Gwydion nudged her away from the edge of the room, and they wove their way through pockets of people. "I definitely prefer going out on a high note, in that case, life blinking away at the height of orgasm. Ending it yourself, when all is said and done."

"Life goals." Kirby laughed. No one ever let her joke about taking her life before. That it didn't faze Gwydion made her feel lighter. Less broken and undesirable.

He pointed them toward the center of the room. "I can't promise the skies will open up, but I can make you sing in pleasure."

"Big words, big guy."

"You keep looking up there." He nodded at a stage that was a few meters away. "Are you curious or envying?"

Kirby's pulse roared in her ears, and desire pricked her skin. "Both."

"Heavy on the envy?"

"Very."

The dais was about a meter off the ground, but as they walked toward it, they climbed invisible stairs. That was her and Gwydion, not a magic in the room.

As they reached the platform and looked over the room, her heart lodged in her throat. She could see everyone who stared up at her. It sent desire racing over her skin.

Gwydion pressed his lips to the shell of her ear again. "Tell me you trust me," he whispered.

"I trust you."

"Tell me I can do whatever I want with you." This time his tone was normal, though it probably didn't carry far.

She liked the possibilities in a request like that. He'd always been more about the pleasure than the pain, but she saw the same scars she had, hidden in his depths. "You can do whatever you want with me."

A bar appeared above her head. Or maybe it had always been there. Gwydion trailed his palms up her arms, to secure her wrists overhead. A flash of memory assaulted her, of her sessions with Starkad. The feeling of his cane across her ass. The unfulfilled desire that taunted her with every session. If she fell too far into those images, she'd get lost in the hurt and rejection.

But it was all background noise. She pushed it aside, to focus on the now. Her body knew good things about being bound this way. About the willing surrender that came with it. And tonight, she had an audience. Gwydion hadn't even touched her intimately, and desire was already pooling between her legs.

"You're so fucking gorgeous." Gwydion glided his hand over the curve of her ass.

Another image flashed in her mind. A vividly potent memory of the first time Starkad spanked her. Of how sore her ass had been the next day. Of how desperately she wanted more pain each time.

Gwydion would give that to her. Darkness licked the edges of her thoughts. He wouldn't deny her anything. The hot slice of steel slicing into her chest mingled with the images of Starkad's whippings. The things she'd do to herself with a razor, for that rush of pleasure.

Gwydion had her knife. If he used it now, could he damage her? Would she feel that delicious high she could lose herself in? Could he make it hurt? Ghosts of pain from her self-inflicted wounds ached across her chest. It had been too long since she felt that sting.

Gwydion rested a palm on her chest, and she gasped at the scalding contact. She was almost panting and hadn't realized her heart was hammering against her ribs until he touched her.

"Your pulse is out of control." He was speaking softly again. A comment meant only for her ears. "Are you okay?"

She wanted to hurt again. To bleed. If he gave that to her, was it the same thing as slipping? As doing it herself? She couldn't form any words. The best she could manage was to stare back with wide eyes. Her brain wouldn't shut up. She didn't want him to cut her, but at the same time she did.

Were the people in the crowd murmuring? Was she losing her shit in front of everyone? No. That was the hammering of her heart against her ribs.

Gwydion brushed a finger over her bottom lip, then tilted her chin, forcing her gaze to his. "Look at me," he commanded.

She nodded.

He traced the faint scars along her chest. She didn't need to look down, to know he followed their path. "I know what these are," he said.

Humiliation seared through her.

"They're a part of you, and there's nothing about you that I don't like, but I won't add to them."

Kirby swallowed past the lump in her throat.

"Tonight, if you scream, it'll only be in pleasure." He trailed his thumb along her cheek. "Are you good?"

She wanted to be. She needed to be. This was part of the mission. Why couldn't she nod?

He cupped her face between both palms. "If you go, I'm going with you this time. And I don't plan on leaving this planet for at least a few more centuries."

His sincerity soothed and warmed her. It didn't matter that he'd never been able to save her before. The promise rang true and quieted her inner demons. Gwydion wanted her for her. There were no demands or judgments here.

"I'm good." She meant it.

"Remember your safeword," he whispered.

Defiance. It made her smile.

If anyone around them was bothered by the delay or the whispered conversation between her and Gwydion, it didn't show in their expressions. Some had turned to other stages, but she still had a captive audience.

With the shadows chased from her mind, lust was free to race in again.

Gwydion glided his hand down her neck, to stroke her breasts through the thin lace of her bra. His movements were deliberate and teasing. Light enough to tantalize. He caressed her nipples. Her neck. Her ass. The inside of her thighs. He stroked each tender patch of skin, until she was swaying against her restraints and her body hummed for more.

When he kissed a path down her breastbone, falling to his knees as he went, she whimpered. Desire licked at the edge of her senses, and climax hovered just out of reach.

He pressed his fingers into the crotch of her panties, and she bucked against his hand, wanting to feel more. The scrape of his teeth over lace made her groan in anticipation. He shoved her panties aside and buried his face in her pussy. Each lick and suck and groan amplified her desire, cranking her anticipation another notch higher.

The relentless attention made her head swim and chased away everything but the *now*. Ecstasy raced over her skin, and orgasm sped up quickly. She screamed when she came, grinding into his face even after his touch was too much.

Gwydion stood and kissed her hungrily, sharing her taste and devouring her gasps. "*Gods*, I love the way you taste. The sounds you make," he murmured against her lips.

She was pretty fond of them too.

He moved behind her. The sound of his zipper was louder and more distinct than any other in the room. He molded himself to her back, his cock digging into her ass cheek.

"I'm so glad you told me *yes* to tonight." His low voice in her ear was rapidly becoming one of her favorite sounds. He reached between her legs from behind and glided his fingers along her slit. "You're the most stunning and deadliest creature here, and no one sees past your beauty. That's a shame." He dipped near her opening, teasing, but didn't enter.

"Subtlety is part of my job." Her reply was breathy.

He pulled back enough to trace the same path his fingers had drawn with the head of his cock. "Not tonight. You should show these pretentious assholes who you are."

"A TOM reject?" That didn't hurt the way it had in the past.

"The last fucking Valkyrie," he growled, as he unhooked her restraints from the bar above her head. "Show them how beautiful you are. Spread your wings. Be *you*."

It was impossible to deny him. The desire to obey was overwhelming. She felt the ground drop away, and they lifted into the air. Light and glitter swirled around them—Gwydion's doing. How much of the show was illusion? It didn't matter. Every eye in the room was on them. She felt it. She wanted to bathe and revel in it.

He slid inside her, and she forgot anyone but them, floating a few feet above the ground as he thrust in and out. "Finger yourself." His command was tangible.

She dipped her hand between her legs, to stroke her clit.

He gripped her hips, and pounded harder with each thrust. The world feel away, and pleasure soared in her chest. She clenched around him as she came again. He spilled inside her, and for that brief moment, they were one.

As he slowed, they descended, until her feet touched the dais. Slowly, the world swam back into view, but she only cared about Gwydion—the way he felt when he slipped out of her, his gentle touch as he adjusted her panties, the caress of his lips along her shoulder blades when her wings faded from sight.

Kirby felt multiple sets of eyes on them as they stepped from the stage. Whispers flitted toward her. Of admiration. Who was she? Could she really be...? No. There were no more Valkyries.

She heard it all, and it heightened the lingering euphoria.

"That's one way to grab the Hooded Spirits' attention." Starkad's voice was dry and flat in her ear.

Fuck him, for trying to kill her buzz, but she needed the reminder. For a few minutes, there hadn't been any prophecies or past lives or gods hunting here. There was only pleasure.

And that was a dangerous way to exist.

She and Gwydion made their way back toward the edge of the room. A flash of something familiar caught her attention. Her mood soured before her brain registered what she was seeing.

One of the waitresses had a body Kirby would recognize anywhere, and the blue eyes that stared back at her, like those of a deer stuck in the headlights, were the same that haunted so many of Kirby's dreams.

What the fuck was Brit doing here?

Chapter Thirteen

Brit was an idiot, to think she'd be done with this covert shit when she walked away from TOM. And here she was, pretending to be wait staff at an orgy for the gods that was supposedly hosted by some of the oldest among them.

She'd pulled a dozen strings, several to the point of severing, to get in the door tonight. Her apron and lingerie didn't hide anything from the guests. At least here, no one was allowed to touch her without asking first. That was a nice change.

It would all be worth it, though. Hel was supposed to be here, and Brit knew how to destroy her. *Fire.* Brit had also spent half the money Starkad gave her on the purchase of a weapon. The pins that held her hair back would become flaming daggers— small, but enough to drive through a god's heart.

And the mask Brit wore did more than cover half her face. It changed the appearance of the bone structure underneath, so she looked like someone else. She just had to hope the disguise held up until she found Hel and executed her.

The goddess took everything from her and would suffer the consequences.

The distinct murmur that swept through the crowd was a sharp contrast to the whispers and moans from seconds earlier. Brit's skin prickled. She followed the turning heads to the center of the main room.

Longing and jealousy joined the tension churning inside, bubbling until they threatened to make her ill. The white mask didn't do anything to hide who Kirby was. She carried herself, knowing the room was watching, and she radiated an invisible strength that was intoxicating even from several meters away.

It figured she'd not only be here, but also as a guest. A twinge of bitterness mingled with the cauldron in Brit's gut.

And Kirby was on Gwydion's arm. Trickster doctor-god, who didn't like to see people in pain? Bullshit. Gods reveled in suffering. Didn't matter who they were.

Where was Starkad? There was no way Brit read his relationship with Kirby wrong.

Brit wasn't missing anything about the sparks that flew between Kirby and Gwydion on that dais— Kirby writhing in ecstasy, with Gwydion practically worshiping her.

Desire thrummed between Brit's thighs, begging for attention.

Would anyone see her or care, if she vanished into a dark corner and relieved the desire that pulsed under her skin? No one was watching her. They were all fixated on the stunning couple who'd just left the stage.

Brit backed away from the crowds. From prying eyes and hands that might want to help. She needed to enjoy this moment herself. No one was here, tucked behind the pillars.

"So much for not seeing me again." Kirby's flat tone cut through Brit's thoughts.

Brit was sick of being phony, especially around Kirby, so all she managed was a tired smile. "Hey."

"Uh huh." Kirby regarded her coolly.

Gwydion's arm was glued around Kirby's waist, and that dagger he carried wasn't a sex toy, or his. Kirby could inflict eons of pain with her mind and make the experience linger—Brit had experienced it firsthand. What the fuck did she need with a dagger?

"I hope you enjoyed the show." Gwydion was easier to read. Distrust and caution spilled from him.

Kirby glanced at him, and the hard lines around her eyes softened. "Do you think Aeval—"

"No." Gwydion snapped off denial. "She's a lot of things, but selling people out after a promise is the kind of karma that even bites a fairy in the ass. And she liked you."

"Excuse me—what?" Brit didn't want to get involved in another conversation like the last time she saw Kirby, where most of what was said went over her head and no one cared to fill in the blanks for her. She'd walk away now—this wasn't why she was here—but Kirby and Gwydion had to be at the party for the same reason she was. So why couldn't she unstick her feet from the floor?

Kirby met her gaze again. "Is this how you define *going your own way*? If you wanted to stalk me, there are easier places to start."

"Stalk you?" Brit had a hard time summoning indignation. She'd considered following Kirby, but the only way to move on was to put the entire past behind her. By pretending Kirby wasn't still alive. By killing Hel. "I didn't know you were going to be here. I'm certainly not interested in watching you fuck someone else." Or she hadn't been, until she saw it. There was definitely more lust than jealousy at the fresh memory.

"Uh huh." Kirby stared at her.

Brit knew better than to talk to fill silence. That was how secrets were spilled. The longer Kirby watched her, the higher the heat cranked under Brit's skin. Why did things have to be like this? Why had she fucked up so many—

Kirby gasped and clawed at her throat, before flying back to collide with the wall behind her. She kicked the empty air, her feet several centimeters above the ground, and fear crept onto her face.

"She's here for me, Valkyrie. As are you." Hel's voice sent ice spilling over Brit.

She reached for the magical weapons pinning her hair in place.

Then every muscle in her body was locked in place.

Kirby refused to panic. She'd been in dangerous situations before. No others where a goddess of death had her pinned to a wall and was crushing her throat and chest, but still... Clawing at the empty air wasn't helping any, so she forced herself to relax. To see if she could grasp any breath at all. If she couldn't, would she die?

Her earpiece sizzled and popped, burning skin, but she didn't have the voice to yelp in pain.

She wanted to sob and cry and give up. She wanted Starkad here, not hissing in her ear, asking what was happening. For once in her life, she wanted to be the helpless maiden someone else rescued.

No you don't. The mental retort surged forward on defiance.

No, she didn't. Gwydion and Brit weren't moving either. It was unlikely Starkad would be any more helpful here, and Kirby knew what she was doing. She was the best. If nothing else, she refused to die on anyone's terms but her own. Especially not Hel's.

"I was pleased to hear you were still alive." Hel stalked forward. Even with Kirby's feet dangling, Hel was taller. "But oh, how far you've fallen from what we tried to make you."

Kirby wanted to retort, or at least spit in Hel's face. She still couldn't draw a breath, though. There had to be a way out of this. She had power. She could break this invisible prison. Couldn't she?

"You were supposed to be a killer. The highest caliber assassin. You're the last Valkyrie." Disdain filled Hel's voice, and her hot breath fell across Kirby's face.

At least she didn't have halitosis. Kirby almost giggled at the out-of-place thought. It was easier than acknowledging the blackness that licked at the edges of her vision and the fear that clawed inside.

Hel shook her head. "You only had to learn a little humiliation. Take your punishment like a good soldier. But you weren't even strong enough to put up with a little feedback. And your life since... You're a whore to those gods no one wants to associate with."

She's right, you know.

Rage surged past hate. Kirby strained against the restraints, struggling despite the fact that her muscles weren't responding. She pushed until her joints ached, and she swore she felt it all the way to the tips of her hair.

"You're weak. You're useless."

Gwydion growled, a low chilling sound, as soothing as it was terrifying.

"Shut it." Hel pointed a finger in his direction but didn't turn from Kirby. "You know it's true. You're not cut out for this. It's why you tried to end things yourself."

Kirby felt a crack, and the grip on her throat loosened. She tried to be subtle about drawing in a deep breath. "You're going to have to try harder than that, to tear me down. My own brain tells me worse shit on a daily basis."

"Hush." Hel's grip was back, tighter than ever. "I'm not done with you. He used to do this to you, didn't he? Back you into a corner? Force you to comply?"

Bile rose in Kirby's throat, carried on doubt and revulsion. Was Hel talking about Mark? Did they know all along?

"You could have learned something from that. At the very least, killed that fucking asshole. But you had to be the martyr." Hel's tone was mocking and disgusted. "Perhaps you liked his hands everywhere."

She was just trying to keep him from subjecting anyone else to the same. The protest wouldn't be forced past Kirby's lips. Why wasn't anyone coming for them? Why hadn't this scene drawn any attention?

Hel clucked. "He certainly wasn't worth trying to kill yourself over. The accusations would have faded. You would have gone back to being in good standing. Or maybe you took the coward's way out because you knew you were never as good as your peers insisted you were."

"*Enough.*" Gwydion shouted. He was loose. Light licked around his skin, brighter than the crystal overhead. The hardwood floor beneath Hel's feet warped and twisted into branches that climbed up her legs and bound her in place.

Gwydion stalked toward her, an anger Kirby had never seen before flashing on his face. "If I have to rip every limb from your body, I'll find a way to destroy you." His low, threatening growl was back.

Kirby nudged her restraints again and felt fissures roll over the layer binding her. The invisible hold shattered, and she dropped to her feet. She rushed toward the chaos to grab the dagger from the inside of Gwydion's arm. Pressed the blade to Hel's throat, applying enough pressure to slice through the goddess's windpipe.

Kirby couldn't break the skin, no matter how hard she leaned her weight into the blade. Hel smirked. The branches binding her legs crackled with ice and shattered, the shrapnel biting into Kirby's flesh.

"*Stop.*" The command reverberated in three overlapping tones, rolling through the ground, and over and through Kirby. It was the most enticing terror she'd ever tasted. She wanted to cower from it, and at the same time wrap herself in its ecstasy.

Three figures in hoods appeared at the edge of the room. "You will not violate our sanctuary this way."

CHAPTER FOURTEEN

Gwydion was fury and destruction, as they stared down the Hooded Spirits. He didn't care which bridges he burned. He hadn't felt this need to obliterate for a cause in centuries.

If this was a hint of what Kirby had faced with TOM, he was no longer so forgiving with Starkad. And Hel... He hadn't summoned the trees in a long time, but if he couldn't kill her, he could plant her in a forest, to suffer for a few decades.

"Out. All of you." One of the Hooded Spirits waved a hand, and Hel vanished, then Brit.

"Wait." Kirby's clear, strong voice pushed aside some of the haze of Gwydion's anger, letting him focus the rest.

The hooded figures turned toward her. "Yes?"

"What Hel just did? That wasn't consensual. She came in here and assaulted us without permission. We were defending ourselves." Kirby looked more fierce than he'd ever seen her, even in nearly no clothing.

"Ah. The *she started it* argument." When the three spoke, their voices were half a beat out of sync, filling the air with a haunting echo. "Yet you came here looking for information about how to destroy her."

Kirby opened her mouth, but the Hooded Spirits spoke over her. "And she tortured you as a child in this life—a life which you only live because, in your first, you stole a soul from death. You're not faulted for defending yourself, but on the rest, we won't offer judgement or opinion."

"Give us some piece of information. You owe me that, after the sacrifices I made on your behalf." Gwydion struggled to shove down enough of his rage to keep it from his voice.

"And this is how your wish to waste that debt?" The echo of voices grew more discordant.

Gwydion nodded. "It's not a waste. Give us this and consider the ledger clear."

The Hooded Spirits approached, and stopped less than a meter away. All three lowered their hoods.

Kirby gasped. Gwydion didn't blame her. He knew what to expect, and the sight still caught him off guard. One was distinctly masculine, with a square jaw and hard eyes. His pale hair was a sharp contrast to his dark skin, and he was aggressively handsome. The second was androgynous. Gorgeous features that didn't lean toward either gender. And the third was a woman more stunning than any other. She looked a lot like Kirby. Not that Kirby would see the same face he did. Each individual saw the Hooded Spirits as what they considered desirable— either to be or to bed.

"If you're looking for Hel's secret weakness or something similar to what defeated Baldur, there isn't one." Watching their lips move while they spoke was more disconcerting than simply listening. Nothing was in sync. "She's a goddess of war and death. Brute force makes her stronger, and kindness may give her indigestion."

Kirby sighed. "But I'm—"

"Question answered. You wanted to know what Hel's weakness was and we've told you. Debt repaid. You'll find your car in its spot at your hotel."

The Hooded Spirits and the mansion vanished, and Gwydion and Kirby were in Starkad's hotel room with him and Min.

Starkad spun to face them, relief flooding his features. "Thank the gods."

Gwydion's fury raced back in force, tinged with futility.

Kirby ripped the destroyed earpiece out and tossed it on the table. "*Hel.*" She couldn't manage any other words. Where was she supposed to focus? On the strange appearance of the Hooded Spirits? She had such a hard time making out their features, but her mind told her they were all beautiful.

She preferred that confusion over lingering Hel's accusations. If Kirby stayed trapped inside those words, she'd tumble into confusion and self-loathing, and she was already struggling to pretend that pit didn't reach out and grab her every time she drifted near it.

"What happened?" Starkad asked.

Kirby could answer that if she could force her mind to stay on the conversation with the Hooded Spirits.

Gwydion met her gaze, and the angry lines around his eyes softened. "What Hel said about your time with TOM... Was it true?"

"Yes." There was no reason to downplay or explain. Hel nailed the reality of it all.

Gwydion's expression hardened again. He whirled on Starkad and caught him with a left cross to the jaw. "You fucking asshole. What the fuck?"

"Ah." Starkad grunted and flexed his jaw.

Kirby understood Gwydion's rage; something similar had been simmering inside since she recovered her past lives. But the resentment was becoming numb. Was it because so much was happening, or was she starting to understand Starkad's reasons for what he'd done? She hated the situation, but she wouldn't be who she was, in this place, with these men, if life had gone differently.

What a fucked-up way to view—her mind gestured vaguely—all of it. The air in the room kicked on, chasing over her skin and sending a chill down her spine. Suddenly the white lacy outfit wasn't enough. She hugged herself. A concrete box wouldn't to keep this feeling out.

Starkad stepped behind her, and a heartbeat later, draped something over her shoulders. She slid her arms into the sleeves one of his button-down and pulled the fabric tight around her. The barely-there scent of sweat mingled with his cologne and the smell of his dryer sheets, wrapping her in security and chasing away the shadows.

"We all made decisions twelve years ago we wish we could take back." Min finally spoke.

Kirby didn't want to live in the past. The bulk of her brain kept drifting to times and places this body had never been, and another chunk of her thoughts was clawing its way back toward the memories Hel had summoned.

"None of that matters. It can't be undone, and if I hadn't been there, others would have suffered the same way. Others did and still are. At least, this way, Hel helped mold the source of her own destruction." She grasped for the strength she needed the words to give her.

Gwydion gently squeezed her arm, and her racing thoughts downshifted. He didn't offer the same kind of safety Starkad did, but she trusted him to stand by her side regardless of the situation, and she'd do the same for him.

"What happened tonight? Did you get what we need?" Starkad asked.

Kirby stalled. Determination wouldn't get her anywhere without knowledge. Her past twelve lives had proven wanting to live and succeed wasn't enough to make it happen. And now she had to put the evening into words.

"Brit was there—I'm sure you heard." Gwydion stepped in, much to Kirby's relief. "She knew Hel would be as well. Hel attacked. The *Genii Cucullati* intervened and banished the us all from the party. They spoke to us first, but..."

Brit... Not the time to dwell on her, but she wouldn't leave Kirby's mind. Kirby appreciated Gwydion's abbreviated version of the encounter. "They told us Hel doesn't have any weaknesses and can't be destroyed, and sent us back here."

"Then we're done." How did Min say that with so much certainty? "It's time to walk away."

Kirby clenched her fists and let the anger flow through her veins, burning everything else away. "All of this, to just give up?"

"We're making a strategic retreat." Min straightened in his seat.

She matched his posture, making her spine ramrod straight. "That was what happened tonight. And now we figure out a new angle and attack."

"We need answers in order to do that." Starkad stepped between them, facing Kirby. "How did Brit know you were there tonight?"

"She didn't." Did Kirby believe that? She'd taken Brit's word so many times, only to have her trust explode in her face. Was Brit okay? It didn't matter right now. "But Hel knew we both would be. She expected us." Compartmentalizing the events, analyzing them for combat purposes, helped Kirby wrap her reactions to them in ice.

Gwydion sank onto the edge of the bed, forearms resting on his knees. "Did she expect you because someone told her you'd be there, or because someone told both us and Brit that was where answers about Hel would be?"

Interesting question. Kirby didn't like the implications, but nothing about this was what it seemed. "That would mean Aeval did set us up."

"Or someone gave her bad information," Gwydion said.

Starkad nudged Kirby toward a chair. She didn't want to sit, but the instant her butt hit the cushion, her energy evaporated.

He took the spot next to her. "Or someone got the information from her or us. It doesn't matter that Hel was there tonight; that's still not her preferred setting. You won't see Min willingly attend a gun show, or Gwydion at…"

"A data-analyst convention?" Gwydion supplied dryly.

Starkad almost smiled. "That. A god avoids their antithesis. It's suffocating. And since she was planning to attack you, if she could have chosen the location, she wouldn't have picked a solstice party."

"Why does any of this matter?" Min slammed his palms on the table, and the joints creaked. "If Hel can't be defeated, we're done. It's not as though tonight was our only effort. We've been doing this for decades."

This was infuriating. Worse than when she tried to convince Min to trust her, in London. He'd always been stubborn, and in past lives she thought that whole domineering, Min-knows-what's-best aura he radiated was sexy. It wasn't working for her now. "That's not the only thing you've been doing. Don't try to wrap it up, all nice and neat, and put a bow on it. You've been fighting this war as much as anyone. Relocating potentials. Giving them their lives back."

"Exactly. I took them out of the line of fire and put them someplace safe."

A rock sank in her gut, weighing her down, as his meaning snaked around her. "You want to stick your head in the sand, then? This would all be better if you could just hide away?" She still couldn't believe Freya made that choice. Gods were selfish, but some of them had to be all right. She glanced at Gwydion. At least one of them was, but that wasn't enough.

"I want people out of the line of fire," Min said. "Starkad is right—I avoid the kind of conflict that involves death. I prefer life and love."

"You knew destroying Hel was the ultimate goal." What could Kirby say to show him what this meant to her?

Min shook his head. "My ultimate goal was keeping you safe. It always has been."

"I'm not safe as long as Hel is out there. As long as anyone who wants to destroy me, us, or potentials is out there. I can't ignore the threat." Kirby refused to let the cancer that was Hel and Loki's desperation spread further.

Min stood, his presence dominating the room, and looked down at Kirby. "You don't have to save everyone. I've hidden myself for centuries, and I can hide you. This can end right now."

"You'd lock me away from the world, to have me to yourself?" Kirby withered at the thought, despite the surge from her past lives saying he was worth it—that *they* were worth it.

"To keep you alive."

Why wasn't he hearing her? She didn't know how to get through to him. "I don't want that."

"And I don't understand why not." Min stepped closer, but Starkad blocked his path.

Kirby rose and held Min's gaze. "That's the problem. I've spent centuries understanding your obsession with making me love you. Over and over. In every life. Yielding to your request that I give you everything. Even though you knew the mere idea of that made me shy away each and every time you asked it, I came to understand. Could you maybe, possibly, just this once, dedicate a month or two to trying to see the world through *my* eyes?"

"I am."

Tension crackled around Kirby. Her every muscle tightened, and she was hyper aware of their surroundings—where each piece of furniture sat, where each man was located, and their posture.

Starkad's said he was as ready for a fight as she was. When did this turn into a battle?

When she felt her choices being stripped away. Again. "Try harder."

"No." Min narrowed his gaze. "You don't respect life, yours or anyone else's, and I can't abide that. I'm trying to understand you, and the more I see, the more it shreds me to the core of who I am."

"So you're suffering?" Sarcasm leaked into Kirby's retort without her permission. "Oh no. No one else here has ever had to do that. I'm sorry my perspective causes you so much pain."

"I'm suffering because you are. Because this causes *you* pain. I would do anything to protect you." Min's deep voice rumbled through the room.

When she was turned on, that tone made her wet. Now, it cranked her tension to full-blown.

"According to your definition of protection. I never asked you to shelter me. To lock me in a box and keep watch over me. I don't want that. I want partners. People who fight by my side and want me to do the same."

"What you want is to destroy yourself. You see enemies around every corner. The way you attacked that waiter in London—"

"You mean the man who murdered your friend?" Her voice rose to match the power in his. "The man who tried to blow us up? Who wanted to kill me?" She was grateful Gwydion and Starkad remained silent. This was one battle she had to win on her own, for her victory to hold power. Why didn't Min understand how important this was?

"The man who had someone to look for, because you won't drop this fight. Because your ghosts haunt you. It's the same reason Hel found you tonight."

Kirby's anger burned, and she swore she felt it lick over her skin. "You think this is my fault? You're going to cast shade for me wanting Hel to stop, after you've spent centuries obsessed with a woman you can't keep alive?" If he was throwing blame around, she'd toss it right back, even though she didn't blame him for a minute for her death in any life.

That he wanted to hold her accountable for what Hel did infuriated her. "You don't love me. You love a memory. You promised your heart and soul and devotion to a series of women who are dead. Not to me. I never asked that of you, and I'm sure as fuck not giving it to you. And if the only reason you're here is to convince the others—to convince me—to pretend the world isn't crumbling around us, I don't want you here."

"M—"

"What?" Kirby glared at Gwydion. She didn't want to snap at him, but if he didn't get where she was coming from. "Are you going to ask me to be reasonable? To think this through? I've been working with faulty information for years. TOM withheld information about the prophecies from me. Starkad didn't tell me where I came from. In the past two weeks, I've had lifetimes of reality dumped on me. I'm expected to process and make the right decisions, based on my entire world being turned upside down. He's asking me to ignore who I am. To give up on taking my life back, and to give it to him instead. Again."

Gwydion shook his head. "I was going to agree with you."

"Huntress." Min stepped toward her, hand outstretched.

She smacked it away. "Don't call me that."

"Kirby, I want to see this through your eyes. I'm asking for the same in return."

She hissed. "Will you help us defeat Hel?"

"No."

Of course not. "Do you understand why I can't let it go?"

"I want to." Resignation rang heavy in Min's voice.

"Yes or no?" Was she shouting?

"No."

A frustrated yell rose in Kirby's chest and emerged strangled. "Then the conversation is over. You said, if I told you to go—if I told you I didn't love you or want your devotion—you'd accept my answer. That you'd leave me alone."

"Please." Min's voice softened.

"I'm telling you to go." It hurt more to say that than she expected. Why? Memories of the past screamed at her to take it back. She was so sick of her past lives controlling her future. "I'm going back to my room. If I see you again, it's because you have a stake in this war that's not tied to your obligation to a ghost. Otherwise, we're done. And I mean that in a very all-encompassing way."

That bit of her past lives stuck her feet to the ground.

Why are you still here? Let's leave.

She knew that voice. It had nagged her since she tried to kill herself. It berated her and tore her down and reminded her how weak she was. It had reveled in the death of the TOM in London. And for once, it was on her side.

She grabbed her purse, which had her room key, and walked out. Her chest tightened when she turned her back on Min, but that wasn't her. The louder voice was cheering her on. The chaos and ache and disappointment and rage threatened to tear her apart from the inside out.

But it was because she chose it.

CHAPTER FIFTEEN

Brit appeared in her hotel room, fury raging inside. It wasn't enough to mask her terror, though. She tossed the sticks from her hair onto the second bed. The weapons had proven useless when she needed them, because she never had a chance to use them.

The events of the party rang fresh in her mind, taunting her at every turn. Kirby's being there should have been a plus. The only high point in a low evening.

Brit yanked off her mask and threw it into a corner.

Except that Kirby looked at her with so much disdain, unlike the adoration she cast on Gwydion. They were happiest, hottest couple in the entire mansion. Maybe Brit should be happy that Kirby wasn't hanging on Starkad's arm instead.

She wasn't.

Brit yanked off the rest of her clothing—what little there was—not caring that she heard several tears in the process. She tugged on the heaviest sweatshirt and baggiest pants she owned. Clothing purchased specifically to curl up and hide in, that had no connection to her past life.

Except she'd bought it with Starkad's money. His bribe, to leave Kirby alone.

Hey. Kirby's ice greeting echoed in Brit's head. It was colder than Hel's invisible prison had been, and nearly as suffocating.

Brit climbed onto the bed and wrapped her blankets around her, but it didn't chase away the chill in her bones.

She'd never seen Hel coming. Even when the bonds broke loose, Brit couldn't get close enough to the brief struggle to participate. Kirby and Gwydion didn't even acknowledge her after Hel arrived.

And why would they? Brit had been helplessly outclassed. A twig in the middle of raging, clashing storms. She'd seen Hel's supposed wrath in school—a tiny explosion here. A snap of pain there.

It was all parlor tricks, compared to what Brit witnessed tonight.

She couldn't do this as a mortal.

You're not weak; you're selfish. Kirby's cold tone echoed in her head.

Kirby was wrong. Compared to beings who could bring wooden floors to life or freeze people in place against their will, Brit was as weak and helpless as a baby.

And unlike Kirby, she doubted some mysterious past was waiting in the back of her mind, to make her immortal and hyper powerful. She didn't have a god and a... whatever Starkad was, watching her back.

176

ALLYSON LINDT

Brit shoved the bitterness aside. She also wasn't the only one who wanted vengeance against TOM. Kirby might have fully enjoyed being fucked in front of a room full of gods, but that wasn't why she'd been at that party. She was both a genuine lover, and a dedicated hunter.

Both things Brit had held against her in the past, and maybe shouldn't have.

The sharp reminder threatened to deter her thoughts, and she dragged her focus back to Hel. Brit couldn't do this alone, but she knew exactly who could help and how to get a hold of them.

Technically, calling Starkad wasn't breaking their agreement. She wasn't pursuing Kirby. True, she hoped it would put them in contact again, but she was offering information to someone she'd shared with in the past.

She swallowed her pride and trepidation, and dialed that familiar number she used to get in touch with Starkad.

As the phone rang over and over in her ear, she winced. Had he dumped the number after all this time? She didn't know why he'd kept it so long, to begin with.

She was about to give up, when his familiar, "Yeah," came over the line.

Brit took a deep breath. There would be no casual conversation or politeness here. "Hey. I'm calling be—"

"Did you know Kirby would be there tonight?" Starkad asked.

If he wasn't fucking Kirby, he wanted to be. There were few things Brit had ever been more

177

certain of. "No. I got intel that Hel would be. I never broke my promise."

"Yet here you are, calling me."

She smooshed down her irritation that his argument matched the one she'd had with herself. "You. Not her. I'm doing it to give you what I have."

"What could you possibly know that we don't?" His disdain oozed over the line.

She faltered. That was a good question. Too late to back out now. "How to defeat Hel."

There was a long pause.

Brit hugged her blankets more tightly around her. Would she ever be warm again?

Starkad finally spoke. "Which is?"

So she did have something he didn't. Her satisfaction was weak. "I'll tell you if I get to be involved in whatever you do with the information."

"No." There was no hesitation this time. "We're not doing this again, where you spoon-feed me morsels and hide your true agenda from me."

"I want Hel gone, so I can move on with my life. There's no hidden motive here."

"There's not? You could have moved on already. That's what the money and ID were for."

Of course there is.

She ignored the thought. "Fine. You don't want what I have? You can go fuck yourself." She disconnected.

Why did he have to be difficult about this?

Why do I?

She snarled at the empty room and burrowed deeper into her blankets.

Min couldn't wrap his brain around the argument with Kirby. Her reasons for pursing this obsession didn't make sense. Why did she think it was comparable to his love for her?

While he didn't look forward to leaving her, he'd promised to go. It was better than being party to this situation. He wouldn't—couldn't—watch her destroy herself or her life. Accidental death was bad enough, but she was pursuing the means of her demise.

Daz was packing Min's luggage. "I hate to see you like this—"

Min knew what came next.

"—but maybe it's time to close this long chapter of your life."

There it was. Daz's ulterior motives lay underneath the comment, the way they always did. Min should mind more. A bit of him was considering the words more closely than he had in the past.

There was an almost overwhelming desire to storm into Kirby's room and demand she hear him out. To do what she challenged in London, and tell her why they always fell in love. That wasn't right, though. She wanted proof, and he hadn't been able to provide that.

Besides, Kirby had made her *no* distinctly clear, and even if she hadn't, he couldn't see this futile mission through her eyes. Which meant he couldn't stay by her side and let her make this mistake.

Daz loaded everything into the car, and they were on their way to the next city over, where Min owned a hotel. They hadn't been able to rouse the pilot on such short notice, but they'd fly out in the next couple of days.

Kirby lingered in Min's thoughts on the drive, and even after they got settled in the new suite. If they were a couple, he'd try again—and again—to make amends. However, that was another part of the problem—he felt like they were, and she didn't.

"Night cap?" Daz's stood in front of him, holding a tray with a two glasses, an ice bucket, and a bottle of bourbon.

Min waved it away. "Thank you, no."

Daz set the drinks aside. "Would you like me to call ahead to Denmark? We can make a stop there. Stay as long as we'd like."

Min's favorite club. A place where the worship flowed freely, and he could have his pick of any woman or man, to bestow his blessing on and ravish in front of the crowds. "I'm afraid I'm not in the mood. Leave me with my thoughts for a while."

"Of course. You need time to process. I understand." Daz took the drinks and stowed them, before leaving for his own room.

Min leaned back on the sofa and scrubbed his face. He couldn't abandon Kirby, but he didn't have a choice. If they'd ended things on a different note…

Then what?

He wouldn't have left.

But he had to say something, to leave the door open for her, while letting her know he wasn't walking through it unless she asked. He pulled a fountain pen and a heavy sheet of cream-colored paper from his briefcase.

She'd told him not to call her *Huntress,* and he stopped himself before he put ink on the page. Sweet salutations were out as well.

Kirby,

I'm at a loss for words, but I find myself needing to write this regardless. I can't promise we'll never see each other again. I assume our paths will cross, whether we intend it or not. However, as you've requested, I will not pursue you romantically.

It ached to write those words, but it was the right thing to do.

This won't stop me from loving—

A memory?

—the woman I fell for, so many centuries ago. I cannot flip a switch and shut off my emotions. If there ever comes a day when you'd like to speak to me, no matter your reasons, I'm not hidden. You can call me or my office or any place associated with me.

I wish you the best of luck in your pursuit, and I hope for your survival.

Your Servant Always,

Min

That was straightforward, yet still respected her wishes.

Min sealed the letter in an envelope that matched the stationary, then again in a plainer one, to keep the first clean and tucked away from prying eyes. He set it on top of his belongings. He'd ask Daz to make sure it made it back to Kirby tomorrow.

For the first time in his existence, Min understood why humans prayed. It was easier to ask a higher power for help, than to admit there was nothing to be done in so many situations.

If he didn't know how the silent pleas worked, he'd try one himself. Beg some deity for Kirby's safety. He didn't want her to destroy herself over this, whether or not she ended up in his arms.

But the only thing he could do now was hope she figured out her path was a mistake before it was too late.

Chapter Sixteen

Kirby's mind was fractured into a million pieces. She should be used to it by now, but these shards were new and unfamiliar. She wanted to hold onto the evening with Gwydion. Each time she managed to grasp the edge of the memory, a warm glow spread inside and her heart skipped.

But everything that came after drowned out the pleasant buzz she should still have.

A shower didn't rinse away Hel's invisible touch. The scalding water wasn't enough to sear her words or Min's from Kirby's mind. She yanked on a T-shirt and panties. It was too much effort to find anything more complicated, and she wasn't going anywhere tonight.

A glance out the window showed her Daz, piling luggage into a car. A moment later, he and Min drove away. So that brief, confusing chapter of her life was over. Min's leaving should be a relief, but parts of her mind argued the decision, loud enough to keep her lingering near the glass until the car vanished into the night.

Kirby wanted to forget it all, but she also wasn't in the mood for a drug-induced sleep or the nightmares that would taunt her regardless. If she couldn't ignore it, she'd dive into trying to control it. Or at least having an impact on some of the outcome.

She grabbed her phone, pulled up copy of the prophecies that Starkad sent her, and flopped onto her stomach on the bed, to read. She'd tried starting at the beginning, but all the words and stanzas blurred together. Most of them didn't mean much without a point of reference. She was using the index instead, scrolling through an alphabetical list and clicking on any keywords that might be relevant.

So far, nothing was panning out. *Eternal Maiden of Death* looked promising. She clicked the link, to go to the correct entry. The flowery verse didn't translate directly to English, but it talked about the eternal maiden of death and her wolf-warrior, defeating a goddess of... Kirby stared at the words. Nope, she didn't know how to translate this. It was *death*, but in a context she didn't recognize.

The lock on her door whirred, and the background noise in her mind shut off. She rolled onto her back, grabbed her HK45C from the nightstand and aimed it at the entryway.

"Don't shoot." Starkad's voice greeted her a heartbeat before he stepped into view.

She shifted her aim to a spot above his head but didn't back down.

He raised an eyebrow. "Should have thought of that sooner. I was trying to be playful and surprise you."

"At least I'm not the only one off my game tonight." She set the gun back on the nightstand. It was tempting to pretend she was pissed off that he'd walked in unannounced. That he had a key to her room in the first place. She didn't mind with him, though, and she'd used up her supply of righteous indignation for the day.

Starkad set a pizza box on the other bed. The scents of pepperoni and oregano made Kirby's mouth water and her stomach growl.

He stood at the foot of the beds, in a casual at-ease stance. Always the soldier. Just like her. "You were certainly on earlier." His tone was light.

A bit more reality horned its way back into her thoughts. He could have been referencing a lot of things, but he meant what she'd done with Gwydion. "Can I help you?"

"You're avoiding me."

Was she? That was ridiculous. They talked. They planned. The other night, they'd had an entire conversation about her in past lives. But she knew what he was talking about. Things didn't feel right between them. "Yes."

"Let's fix that."

We can't fix this. You can't just barge in here and force me to talk. Those and a series of other flippant answers rushed to the tip of her tongue. She was too tired to spit any of them out. And she missed what she had with Starkad before everything fell apart. Sure, she'd been torturing herself, lusting after a man who didn't return the sentiment, but she'd known it. Life was comfortable. "I don't know how to talk to you anymore."

"Ah." He settled on the edge of her bed.

"That's the best you've got? No neutral retort? No *same as always*?"

Starkad studied her with a reserved expression and the piercing gaze she'd built entire fantasies around.

Today, his silence summoned waves of repressed frustration, that surged into her thoughts so she didn't know where to focus.

"I remember who we used to be, in my first life," she said. "*Gods*, I loved you. I'd have to. Wouldn't I? To defy Odin the way I did? And a month ago, I knew where we stood. I desperately wanted your attention, and I hovered on that edge between being convinced you wanted me too but refused to admit it, and thinking you only tolerated me out of some sense of obligation."

Creases appeared on his brow. He still wasn't going to talk?

Fine. She wasn't done, anyway. "And now I get it. I understand where you were coming from. But it still fucking hurt. The rejection. The denial. The lack of answers. I want to move past that and forgive you, but I can't. I definitely don't want to go back to what we were, even if it was predictable, but I also don't like cutting this wide path around you. The bad of what you did doesn't outweigh the good." Did it?

Starkad still didn't respond.

Kirby's anger spiked. "Say something, damn you." She barely avoided shouting the demand. "Don't do this to me. Don't get me to spill my guts to fill empty air. Tell me what's on your fucking mind. For once in this gods-damned fucking life, tell me what you're thinking, instead of shutting me out *for my own good.* Please?" She hated that she ended with a whimper.

He sighed.

She clamped her jaw shut so tightly it ached.

"I don't regret fucking you in Salt Lake," he said.

Relief fluttered inside, threatening to push out a sob. She remained passive.

"I do regret that I lost control."

"You mean actually letting how you feel show?" Bitterness lined her question.

"Yes."

A tiny little cheerleader was dancing and shaking her pompoms in Kirby's skull at the confession he felt *something.* "And?"

"What makes you think there's more?"

So. Fucking. Infuriating. "I just *begged* you to be honest with me. If that's the only thing you're holding back, nothing will be right with us ever again."

"If I keep going, the pizza will get cold." His expression finally shifted to a dry smile. *Fucker.*

She rolled her eyes. "Fuck the pizza."

He closed the distance between them and leaned as close as was possible without making contact. "I'd rather fuck you." His voice was a low growl. "Listening to you with Gwydion tonight was torture, and I didn't like being on the receiving end. But you knew that."

"Let's say I hoped." Her pulse roared in her ears, and all the pent-up emotions rushed into a new outlet. "I've never been certain you noticed."

"I see all of it. The low-cut tops. The nude sunbathing. I *do* want you. Marked and whimpering for more pain. Naked underneath me. I used to beat myself raw, jerking off after our sessions. I still fantasize about doing things differently, just once. Shoving my fingers between your legs. Stroking your pussy until you come. Fucking you until both of us forget the world around us. *You.* Not Ruby."

This didn't solve anything. Sex never did. She used it as an escape. Except the electricity that licked over her skin and the way her pulse hammered in her hears insisted this was different.

So did her heart. "If we do this, you have to promise me something." She forced strength into her voice.

"Anything."

"Don't give me that so easily. Not until you know what I'm asking for." Kirby ached for this to be a new step in their relationship, but she didn't trust it. She did trust a promise from Starkad. He kept secrets, he blurred the lines of truth, but if he swore something, he meant it.

"It doesn't matter." His breath was hot against her skin. "I told you I want to make this right. *Anything.*"

"That tonight is a beginning and not an end. That we talk when this is over. That you stop shutting me out." She wanted him so very much, but she wouldn't go through another round of his regret and her despair.

Starkad tilted up her chin with his finger. "You know it's not that easy."

"You said *anything.*"

188

"And I meant it. I'll give you what you're asking for, but we both have a lot of bad habits to break. There are going to be some stumbles. I'll make mistakes. So will you."

Kirby was okay with that. She might not be when it happened, but she expected it to be a difficult process. "Okay. Then one more thing."

"You're killing me. But okay." His reply was gravel.

She leaned in and bit his bottom lip, earning herself a dangerously tantalizing growl. "Don't be gentle."

He tugged at her T-shirt, and a loud *rip* rushed to her ears. The fabric burned with delicious friction across her skin when he tore away the top. The hunger in his eyes made her whimper in anticipation. He bit her shoulder hard enough to mark her, and she groaned into the lingering pain.

A sliver of her was terrified he'd stop at any moment. Push her away and tell her this was a mistake.

He promised. And she trusted that.

He pinned her to the mattress and wedged a knee between her legs. His touch was rough, as he kneaded her breasts and pinched her nipples. Any restraints that kept them apart in the past had fallen away.

She shifted her ass on the bed, to rub her mons against his leg. He bit a nipple harder. The grinding and groping built to a frantic pace. If she adjusted her position—if he pinched something new—would she come?

He pulled back, gripping her hips hard to stop the thrusting. "No." Before her disappointment could settle in, he tore off her panties. "Not yet. Kneel on the bed, back to me."

"Yes, sir." She could barely hear herself over the roar of her pulse in her ears. She heard the buckle on his belt, and her body reacted, moisture coating the inside of her thighs.

Hand between her shoulder blades, Starkad pushed her onto all fours. He glided his palm over her ass, his touch so light she barely felt it. He pulled away, and nothingness rushed in.

Pins and needles of expectation prickled her skin.

The whistle of his belt sliced the air, and leather slapped against one butt cheek. Kirby gasped at the shock. *Fuck*, she'd missed this.

Starkad alternated, striking one side and then the other, laying down the lashes to mark her. She clenched her jaw, to keep from crying out and startling anyone in the adjoining rooms. Bliss sank in, blurring the lines between where one strike stopped and the next started, and her thoughts fuzzed at the edges.

By the time the belt dropped next to her on the blanket, she was panting with desire. Her chest clenched with the reminder of what always came next. Starkad's soothing the wounds, then rocking her to sleep. Neither of them getting off until they went their separate ways the next morning.

Her heart soared when he kissed and bit lightly up her spine, and shoved his hand between her legs. His fingers penetrated her without further warning, but she was so wet, there was little friction.

She sobbed with relief and pleasure. From this angle, he wouldn't hit a sweet spot to make her come, but the way he filled her with a touch, and the lingering stings on her backside, stole her thoughts and kept her wrapped in a cloud.

He moved his fingers to her clit, pushing her to the edge, then pulling away as her body started to clench.

He repeated the teasing, over and over, until she was lost in need. "Please?" She didn't have the capacity for more words.

His touch vanished, and her heart jammed in her throat. Then his fingers were back, stroking her clit, pressing in hard. Not easing up when she bucked against his hand, climax washing over her.

Starkad grabbed her shoulder and shoved her onto her back. He pinned a hand to her throat, gaze locked on hers. "Better?" he asked.

"Yes, sir." *Gods*, yes.

His smile was one she'd never seen before. It carried unspoken promises that were almost enough to make her come again. He managed to undo his trousers with one hand, knelt between her legs again, and thrust his cock inside her.

He hammered hard and fast, skin slapping against skin, while he pressed on her windpipe just enough to further fuzz her thoughts. The frantic need behind it all pushed her into another orgasm. She was lost in the clouds when he peaked, spilling inside her.

He let her stay in the pleasant buzz, his touch turning tender as they slowed to a stop.

This was all so perfect. It made a whisper of terror linger in the back of her head and heart. Not of what they'd done—that was incredible and so worth the wait—but of how far inside her heart Starkad was.

She'd trusted him for years, but this was a whole new level of *close*. One they didn't even have in her first life. She didn't know how to define it, but it scared the fuck out of her.

CHAPTER SEVENTEEN

Kirby hovered in a pleasant haze of post-coital bliss. Starkad was gentle after the sex, helping her clean up and taking care of her, the way he always had. It didn't matter that they were in her room; he gave her his shirt, to make up for ripping hers.

It smelled like him and soothed her soul further. She pulled his arms tighter around herself as they sat on the bed. If she went to sleep, would this all vanish when she woke up?

He promised it wouldn't.

"I think the pizza got cold." His chest rumbled against her back when he spoke.

She smiled. "I told you it would. Why did you bring it?"

"I wanted to hang out. To spend time with you without the walls up."

If only a bit of rough sex and some verbal foreplay were as effective as a wrecking ball. "The walls are still there."

"Then let's start building some ladders over them."

Cheesy line. She liked it. "I used to do this with Brit—order takeout in the hotel, be silly, screw." And just like that, she'd jumped off a cliff into the awkward territory of bringing up the ex. It didn't sting the way she'd expect it to.

"I didn't mean to summon trigger memories."

She laughed at his wording. Her recovered memories were behind so much of this. "That's exactly what you meant to do. Maybe not tonight, but you've been pushing for that—"

"No, I haven't." Starkad's voice was firm.

True. She'd made an unfair accusation. He'd specifically kept her away from Gwydion for years, to keep her from remembering before she was ready. Correction, before Starkad thought she was ready. But they were moving past that. She leaned back, to rest on his shoulder. "I don't want to talk about Brit. I have three immortal men vying for my attention, and at least one and a half of you are trying to see this from my perspective."

"I take it I'm the half?" Starkad asked dryly.

She turned her head to the side, to look at him. "Five eighths. No one's perfect."

He rolled his eyes and brushed his lips over hers. "I appreciate the concession."

"Damn straight, you do." Everything about this felt so right.

"If you don't want to get into… her, you pick what you'd like. What's on your agenda, besides enjoying this finest of cold gourmet pizza?" Starkad managed to reach over to the other bed, to grab the box, without completely displacing her. He straightened again and set the food in front of her.

She was reluctant to leave his embrace behind, but a little eye-contact would do her some good. And make it easier to eat. Her stomach was growling again, now that the intense sex-hunger was sated. "I want to do something we've never done before."

"Oh?"

She knew so little about him. There were the memories of their few times together—who he was in each one, and like he'd said about her, who he was at his core was always the same. He knew so much about her, though.

"Tell me a story about your life. Happy. Sad. Anything." *Just show me you've done more than pine for me for more than a thousand years.*

"Ah."

Kirby was going to smack him if he kept doing that. Rather than launching into another tirade to fill the silence, she grabbed a slice of pizza and took a huge bite. It was pretty good, even at room temperature.

She nudged the box toward him with her knee, and finished off the first slice in record time. Two bouts of marathon sex broken up by fights with a goddess and two exes made her hungry. She took the second piece more slowly, plucking off a few pieces of pepperoni to eat by themselves.

"Would you like to know why you never found me when you were in Kuwait? After?" A hint of somberness mingled with his light tone.

It snagged Kirby's attention. "I would." She, Gwydion, and Min had tried to reach him back then. It wasn't as easy as dropping Starkad an email or text, but Min and Gwydion had connections, and not a single one could point them in a direction.

"I'd decided not to look anymore." Starkad's words were like a knife to the heart.

So much for wanting to hear he hadn't been obsessing.

Starkad saw Kirby's hurt. Then again, he almost always did. He was glad he'd come here. There was going to be a lot of pain involved, but it felt good to finally move past the secrets. "The thing is ignoring their calls was devouring me. I couldn't forget you. I was trying. But I had to know, if I walked back into your life, I wouldn't lose you again."

"I was kind of hoping for a story about how the all-consuming love waned for a little bit." She was smiling again, though.

Worth it. "Okay… 1692."

"Oddly specific."

And he remembered every detail of that time of his existence. "To catch you up, from when you died the first time—Odin destroyed Ruby, and I lost my shit. I fought in every conflict I could find, hoping to discover that I wasn't actually immortal after all."

"I can't imagine what that's like," Kirby said sarcastically.

He'd called her reckless and self-destructive so many times, but he'd been there too. The feeling had faded enough with time that hindsight let him see his actions weren't the smartest, but she was still coming out the other side of being stuck in the middle.

"I either wanted vengeance or to be destroyed, finding it," he said.

"I feel like someone just walked over a dozen of my graves." Kirby shivered and rubbed her arms.

Starkad started in on a piece of pizza, using it as an excuse to collect his thoughts. "Odin said you'd be reborn again and again, but what were the odds I'd be the one to find you? I only had his vague curse to go on. Would you be mortal? Norse? What would you look like? I had no idea his less-than-detailed damning would yield such specific results. I swore I saw you during the Battle of the Trees, but I couldn't find you again. I figured you were either dead again, or a ghost, taunting me by keeping me safe."

"The truth isn't nearly so noble," Kirby said.

The Battle of the Trees was when she met Gwydion for the first time, and that war was the stuff of legends. "It didn't matter how many battles I fought. How many should-be-fatal wounds I suffered. I was still here, and you weren't."

"Wow."

This was harder to fall back into than he thought. None of these thoughts occurred to him when he was watching Kirby struggle after he pulled her out of TOM. Now the parallels between how he dealt with losing her and how she dealt with Brit's betrayal were painfully clear. "You have drinks in the fridge?"

"Always do."

Starkad made his way to the mini fridge tucked under the counter. "Water or cola?"

"Water."

He grabbed himself a cola and a water for her. "Heads-up." He tossed her the bottle.

She snagged it out of the air without fumbling.

He cranked the lid off his drink and downed half of it in a single gulp. The delay didn't help him assemble his thoughts. He leaned back against the counter. "It all blurred together as science and art advanced, and suddenly no one wanted a crazed warrior fighting with them. The gods were stories, and a berserker... I was just a word. There were no others like me left. People wanted knights and meat shields. I was tired. Looking for a new purpose. And I was friends with a wonderful woman in Rome. She didn't care that I was a little... uncivilized. And she was nothing like you."

Kirby frowned.

"Don't be hurt." He returned to the bed and sat next to Kirby, his leg pressed into hers. "I thought I wanted *docile* and *timid*. Someone to tame and domesticate me. She and I talked about marriage. I told myself she was what I needed, to reset my place in the world. She had money and prestige. Introduced me to so many people in high society."

"Sounds positively... lovely?" Her doubt was mild, compared to what his had been at the time.

"I was withering from the inside out. And I thought I should be. That was what normal people did. Until one night…" The centuries after Ruby's death were a giant blob of battles, but that party in Rome was vibrant. The colors. The scents. The flavors. Her familiar laugh.

"It was a party for her father's associates. Some of the gods had adapted. Blended in. They moved through society like anyone else. One of them was there. His Italian was horrible. Kept slipping into Celtic. He captivated the room with his jokes and stories. People migrated to him." He looked at Kirby. The same face in every life. The same voice. But never quite the same woman. I was more interested in the stunning woman on his arm."

She gasped. Her eyes were wide. "That was… Oh geez."

Starkad nodded. "At the time, I told myself there was no way it was you. She was another ghost, haunting me for falling for someone else. Mary Margaret and I went home. I tried to forget about you." He'd fought so hard to shove the evening to the back of his mind. To force it to blur with rest of his past. "The longer I thought about it, the more I convinced myself it was you. The nagging grew over days and then weeks."

"I didn't know who I was." Kirby picked at the blanket. "I had an amazing Welsh boyfriend, who doted on me and worshiped me. Then I saw you at that party, and everything started to fall apart in my head. He was sympathetic. Had a doctor look at me. But they didn't know what was wrong. Why I was hearing things. Seeing things. Had horrible headaches. Gwydion wanted to take me out of Rome before someone decided I was possessed. He was going to take me to a specialist." Pain rang in her words. "I died—was killed—on that trip."

Starkad would find that out later. "I reached a point where I couldn't think about anything but that party. I told Mary Margaret that she deserved someone who would love her as much as she loved me, and I left to find you. By the time I caught up to Gwydion, you were gone. He told me he'd had another life with you and introduced me to Min. We put the pieces together."

"And hello, eternal search for a pretty blonde." Kirby's voice cracked.

Starkad rested a hand on her thigh. "It wasn't like it had been before, but finding you again did change my perspective. It proved you were out there, and that I hadn't forgotten about you, the way I hoped."

She leaned against his arm, her head on his shoulder. "I thought tonight was going to be death number thirteen. When Hel pinned me to the wall… I was certain she was going to kill me. No. She just wanted to torture me a little. Cut my wounds open. Rub salt in them. Tell me I should have killed Mark. That she was waiting for me to do exactly that at the academy."

"She would have punished you for it. They would have made you suffer regardless." Because that was what Starkad hadn't seen. One of his bigger mistakes. If Hel and Loki either broke Kirby or made her theirs, she wouldn't kill Hel, the way the prophecies said.

"But she has a point."

"That's wouldn't be you, though. You put yourself on the line for others. It's never been about saving yourself."

She relaxed against him. "I brought *you* back for selfish reasons."

"I thought you did it for me."

"I did it for us. I couldn't imagine life without you," Kirby said.

"And now we each understand how the other feels." Starkad sighed. "It only took us a thousand years to get back to this point."

She laughed dryly. "That's nothing, in the span of eternity."

But having her here was everything. And he couldn't lose it—her—again.

CHAPTER EIGHTEEN

The longer Brit sat in bed, huddled under the blankets and letting the night play on a loop in her head, the more her muscles tightened and protested.

She wasn't falling asleep anytime soon. If The Hooded Spirits knew where to send her, who else could find her here? Did she need to move hotels? Was Starkad going to send someone after her, for breaking her promise?

It wouldn't be Kirby, so it didn't matter, on so many levels.

And if ancient gods could find and send her anywhere, was there a point in hiding?

She wouldn't be this stressed if Starkad had agreed to her terms. She wouldn't be this stressed if Mark were still here.

Her gut revolted. She'd be an entirely different kind of *stressed*. Just because his presence was familiar and kept her from being alone, didn't mean it was something to miss.

Brit didn't like this isolation, though. The reality jarred her in a way she didn't want to ponder.

Living in the dorms, in the officer apartments, she'd always been surrounded by people who had her back.

Why did Starkad turn her down? She had good intel to share. She'd provided him with reliable information for years, and that asshole had the nerve to tell her he didn't want her help. He had the balls to tell her she was selfish. He was as bad as Kirby had been on the plane, refusing to accept Brit's apology or give her any closure at all.

Brit had done so much for them. Even before she discovered Kirby was still alive. They owed her.

And Starkad paid. Cash and a new life. Just like you asked.

She winced at the internal argument.

I helped them to help me. To get me out of that place. To save my ass.

Sure, that was part of her goal, but she could have left in other ways. Instead, she chose to right the wrongs she'd been trained into.

I'm not that selfless. I was eliminating those they might send after me.

No. They didn't send TOMs after TOMs.

They let Mark and I stay to eliminate Kirby. Would they really tell me if that was standard operating procedure?

Yes. Because Brit would be the one doing the hunting. She'd been their best sniper.

Besides Kirby.

Wrong. Brit shoved back on the argument with conviction. She might be doubting a lot of things, but even Kirby knew Brit was the best sniper TOM had.

Why wasn't that enough? Why wasn't I enough?

The voice in her head wasn't hers anymore; it was Kirby's. Great. Now Brit was having imaginary arguments with the woman who didn't love her or want anything to do with her.

Because you betrayed me.

This was worse than talking to herself. Brit threw the blankets off, suddenly too warm and constricted. The world was closing in around her, squeezing the air from her lungs and gripping her mind in an ever-tightening fist.

Did you see me tonight? So happy on his arm? You and I used to have that.

Brit definitely didn't like this Kirby-voice, living in her head.

Before you picked a little extra security over me. Over us.

It was more than *extra security*. Mark had tortured Brit. Bullied her. Raped her.

And we would have stopped him together. You just had to say something.

"*You never did,*" Brit screamed in the empty room. "You left me alone."

Someone hammered on a shared wall, jarring her. Why was she so hot? She needed to get out of these clothes, but she didn't want to. They were comfort and safety. No one else gave her that. She had to find it herself.

She stumbled into the bathroom, humming loudly in her head, to drown out Kirby's voice, and cranked the water on as cold as it would go. The cold spray hit her face first, numbing her skin but not her thoughts. The water pounded against her body and clothes, soaking into the fleece until the fabric hung heavily on her frame.

Brit let the weight drag her to the floor of the tub. The shower beat against her, steady and predictable, and giving her a beat outside of her head to focus on.

The heat evaporated, replaced with an icy sensation that clawed over her skin. Now she was thinking about Hel again. *Fuck.* She tried to sob, but she was too tired. Too cold.

She hugged herself more tightly, and clenched her jaw to keep her teeth from chattering. No one was coming for her. There was no lust-worthy authority figure to walk into her room and cradle her. No one to strip her out of the wet clothes, then dry and comfort her.

Kirby would have done all that for her, but she was gone. Because Brit was a coward.

Because your own life matters to you more than anyone else's. Survival instinct, bitch.

Great. The Kirby voice was still here. And if what she said was true, why had Brit let Mark get away with so much?

Because his torment was predictable. Routine. Because you were terrified of it getting worse.

Brit couldn't be blamed for that.

You can if it means you sold me out. Remember? The woman you swore you loved?

Reality crashed around Brit, and her body shook with the cold. She'd fucked up so bad. There was no way to make this right. She'd been selfish, egotistical...

And she pushed Kirby away, because Kirby was above that kind of bullshit.

Because she's a perfectly self-righteous—

No. Brit silenced her own mental voice. Kirby had flaws, the same way Brit had good points.

Maybe it's time to let me off this pedestal.

Maybe.

Brit pushed to her feet on wobbly legs. It might also be time to stop pretending she had any possibility of being effective in this fight. She changed the water to lukewarm, to keep from shocking her system, and stripped out of the soaked clothes.

When she could stand without shaking, she turned off the shower and rubbed herself dry.

There were two things she could do, to help Kirby and take out Hel. Her gut wrenched at the thought of both, because she didn't know how she'd survive.

So you'll be a martyr?

No. In fact, her plan would probably leave her as the forgotten body in the unmarked grave, and every bit of her instincts fought against the idea. But this wasn't about her. Brit had wrongs to right, with Kirby and with the damage she'd helped TOM do— not just the path of death they left scattered across the world, but also the recruits they created. People like Brit and Mark.

Acid churned in her stomach and surged up her throat, as she dressed. A funeral dirge sang in her thoughts. It was better than listening to fake-Kirby berate her.

She banished the whisper of self-pity. These were her decisions, and they were the right ones, whether or not she liked them.

But she had to sleep first. She'd never cared for the TOM-approved regimen of *drugs to fall asleep, drugs to wake up*. There was no way she could relax without them tonight, though, and she needed to be on her game to do this. If Hel was feeling vindictive, Brit may not get the chance to rest again for a while.

Brit didn't feel refreshed, necessarily, but she was ready to put her plan into motion. Easy part first, as a primer.

She called Starkad.

What if he doesn't pick up? She should have considered that sooner.

"I haven't changed my mind since last night," he answered.

Was it her imagination, or was a layer of the gruffness gone? "I have. I don't know much, but I'll give you what I have."

"In exchange for…?"

"Nothing." Brit felt lighter. "You're already doing the one thing I want—taking care of Kirby."

"How do I know this is legitimate?"

"You don't. I didn't either. But it was the best I could find, and it cost me a lot." Not everything. Not yet.

"What are you up to, Brit?"

She smiled at the receiver. "Hel's weakness is fire. I'm sorry I don't know more. Good luck." She disconnected.

The next bit was harder. She shouldn't do this—her sacrifice should be completely altruistic—but she needed Kirby to know. Not until it was all over, though. Not before Brit executed the rest of her plan.

It was so Kirby wouldn't go through life feeling bitter.

Liar. It's so she won't go through life hating me.

That would be unavoidable, but this might soften the blow. And yeah, it was as much selfish as anything. Brit was willing to admit it.

After her explanation and a little extra information for Kirby were recorded, Brit encrypted the message. She had a secure channel she used, to send Starkad mission briefings, and she set everything to deliver based on the same trigger Hel had in place. If it never sent, it meant Hel won.

Please let it send.

When she was done, Brit pulled the SIM from her phone and destroyed the card. It was time to obliterate all of her ties to the past except one. The thought was as freeing as it was terrifying. Was this how Kirby felt, leaving it all behind?

Brit grabbed the handset for the phone in her room and dragged in a deep breath. Once she did this, Kirby would never forgive her. It would probably kill Brit.

Her mind screamed at her to stop.

She steeled herself and dialed the number that acted as a routing point for all calls going into TOM.

"Thank you for calling The Order of Mistletoe," a chipper voice answered. "How may I direct your call?"

Bile rose in Brit's throat, and she cringed. "I'd like to speak with Hel, please." Her tone was professional and calm, defying the chaos in her head.

"I'm sorry. There's no one here by that name. Are you sure you have the right number?"

Brit was certain. "Tell her Brit is on the line."

"I see. Please hold." Like that, the receptionist's tone turned hard.

The music was gratingly pleasant. Piano renditions of classical scores, punctuated by a message every fifteen seconds, telling her that her call was important, and to please remain on the line.

Hang up, her mind screamed.

"Flight of the Bumblebee" played in her ear.

Hang up now.

She couldn't.

I can. Vanish. Stay safe. No one ever has to see me again.

She had to see this through.

Why? No one will ever know but me.

It didn't matter.

Hang up.

Brit hovered her fingers over the button that would disconnect the call.

Hel came on the line. "Corporal."

Brit's heart dropped into her stomach at the title she should have been stripped of when she deserted. . "Sir."

"What can I do for you?"

This part was easy. Brit just had to reach inside a little ways, summon recently buried thoughts, and let her terror leak through in the process. "Forgive me. Please. I made some stupid mistakes. I let seeing Kirby again cloud my judgment, and I was wrong. I've only ever wanted to serve The Order. The party, looking to hurt you for her, it was a mistake. I know where my loyalties lie."

The line went dead. What was she supposed to do with that?

"I know what you are. We trained you." Hel's voice came from directly behind.

Brit spun to see the goddess standing directly behind her—statuesque, stunning, and terrifying.

Hel tilted Brit's chin up to meet her gaze. "I won't forgive you because you spin a few pretty words."

It was easy to fall into old patterns and submission in Hel's presence. Brit tried to pull away, to stare at the ground, but Hel held her face in place.

"I don't expect proving my loyalty to be easy"—she let the quaver slide into her voice—"I'll do anything to get back at Kirby. For humiliating me. For killing my partner. But I'm too weak to do it without you."

Hel clucked. "Kirby was such a disappointment, but you… You've always excelled. I was hurt to hear you left us for her."

"I would never. I was trying to get into her good graces. To tell you—"

"Don't spin that double agent bullshit with me. I know why you were at that party, and I know who shot your partner."

"I was wrong. Not about Mark"—she refused to take that back—"but thinking I wanted to leave. Whatever I have to do to show you I'm sincere, I will."

Brit would grovel and suffer and walk through torment, to earn Hel's trust. To fight by her side against Kirby. If there was any chance left for her and Kirby, this would destroy it.

But Brit wanted to see TOM burn to the ground and take Hel with it, and the best way she could think of to do that was by joining Hel, and then betraying her.

CHAPTER NINETEEN

Gwydion had grown accustomed to waking up with Min nearby. Same room. Same city, at least. Not that Min's presence was a constant, but it was odd, knowing that by staying where Kirby was, he might not see Min again for a long time.

Not that he doubted her decision; the new way of things would just take adjusting to.

He knocked on Starkad's hotel room door. This would take adjusting as well—the top-secret meetings, hidden away in rooms, instead of going out in public and having casual conversations.

When Kirby answered, wearing a lazy smile, Gwydion's musings evaporated.

"Morning." She brushed her lips over his in what had to be the sweetest, most chaste kiss in history, and stepped aside to let him in. "I'm sorry if you're missing your travel companion."

Something was different here. "I appreciate it, but it's okay. I understand why you did it, and I agree. I also brought coffee." He handed her one of the cups of coffee he'd brought.

She took a sip and sighed. "It's going to be a while before coffee holds the same spark for me, after Aeval's. And this is why I'm not interested in *The Best* sex ever."

"Point taken." Gwydion looked past her, to see Starkad roll his eyes, but the berserker was smiling.

Really fucking odd. Almost creepy. In a funny way. He set Starkad's drink on the table, grabbed his own, and settled into a chair. "When you're ready for breakfast, I know a few places."

"Maybe later." When Kirby walked past Starkad, he brushed his fingers over hers, before she sat between him and Gwydion.

Gwydion rarely traveled with Starkad. And it had never been when Kirby was alive. He liked seeing the two of them like this, especially since she wasn't pulling away from him. She leaned back in her wooden chair and rested her feet on Gwydion's legs.

The last few days had taught him this wasn't Kirby and Starkad. The tension in the room was lighter than it had been since they arrived. "Something's changed."

"Everything's changed." Starkad's tone was somber. "It's why we're here."

Yeah, yeah. Always the wall of stoicism. But Kirby didn't mask her feelings. A light smile played on her lips.

The two of them were adorably disgusting. "You fucked, didn't you? Screwed and made up?" Gwydion didn't have a problem calling them on it.

"*Made up* implies a huge chasm was crossed. This was more of a medium-sized chasm." Kirby sipped her coffee.

Gwydion couldn't help himself. "I've seen him naked. It's pretty huge."

Starkad clenched his jaw. He didn't summon the irritation as well as normal. "Could you two—"

"Wait. Really?" Kirby dropped her feet to the ground and leaned in. "You've seen…" She nodded at Starkad.

"Why would I make that up?" Gwydion asked.

Starkad opened his mouth again. "I have—"

"Are we talking about standard guy reasons for seeing people naked? Showers at the gym? Urinal? Or something more?" Kirby set her drink down and leaned in, as if she was waiting for gossip.

"Definitely more." Perhaps today wasn't the right time for that revelation, but Gwydion was tired of secrets.

"—information about—"

"*Hot*." Kirby cut Starkad off. "*Wow*, the mental images. Just so you know, my imagination is working overtime now."

Gwydion gave her a mock bow. "Always happy to be of service."

"I have information about defeating Hel," Starkad barked.

"Oh." Kirby's smirk evaporated, and she let out a long breath.

"You should have led with that," Gwydion said.

Starkad fixed him with a glare. "Are you fucking with me right now?"

"No, but at least two of us are interested later." One more jest wouldn't hurt anyone.

The lightheartedness was gone from Kirby's laugh. "Where did you get information between tonight and this morning?" It made sense she'd be all business again. The soldier in her wouldn't allow anything else.

Gwydion wished he didn't get it, but he did.

"Brit," Kirby said when Starkad didn't answer.

Gwydion had missed something. "Why would you guess her?"

"Because he doesn't hide his sources when it's anyone else. What happened to her staying out of my life?" She was focused on Starkad.

Starkad slapped his fingers against the side of his cup, not drinking, just abusing. "She's struggling with that. The first call was a bunch of bullshit about regret and not being able to use the information by herself. Swearing she didn't know you'd be at the party. Insisting she be allowed back into your life if she gave me this."

"Ah." Kirby managed to cram a liter of bitterness into a single syllable. "Wait. When was the first call?" She dropped her feet to the ground.

Starkad winced. "Last night. I didn't want to spoil the evening."

Wanted to get laid. Gwydion didn't blame him.

"Second one was about fifteen minutes ago. I wanted to share with everyone," Starkad said.

"Completely different tone. She didn't ask for anything. She just handed over what she had and wished us luck."

"That doesn't sound suspicious at all." Kirby bounced her knee to a frantic beat. Was she talking about Brit's change of heart, or Starkad's withholding information about the conversations?

An argument that would have to wait. Preferably until Gwydion wasn't caught in the middle, because he'd take Kirby's side, and that would come with a whole new layer of friction. "What's this supposed wondrous secret?"

"Fire. Supposedly Hel is weak against fire."

That actually made sense. So many gods of the afterlife kept parts of their realms cloaked in fire and brimstone, but the Norse gods tended to be more about the storms. Rain. Thunder. Snow. And Hel was the ultimate ice queen. "I assume we don't believe her."

"We don't have anything else. The Hooded Spirits told you Hel has no weaknesses," Starkad said.

The air changed, unpleasant sparks racing over Gwydion's skin. Something was wrong. Something magical and malevolent was nearby.

"They did say that." Kirby hopped to her feet, rubbing the insides of her wrists. "But we have the prophecies. The ones that say we kill her. Do we put any faith in those? I wanna get out of here. Should we go? Get breakfast or something? I want French toast with strawberries and bananas. Can we get that here?"

"Probably." Gwydion was only half-focused on the Hel conversation. The change in the hair had Kirby on edge, too. Something was wrong, and he didn't know what.

Kirby bounced on the balls of her feet. "Let's go get breakfast. In France."

"They don't actually serve French toast in France. You know that." Starkad was sitting straighter. He felt it as well.

Kirby took a few steps toward the door, then drifted back. "Crepes, then. Sweet. Savory. It all sounds good. I'm hungry. Why won't she stay gone?"

Starkad's jaw was tight, as he looked at Gwydion. "How quickly can you be ready to leave? As in, town."

"Five minutes if I have to prep. I can go now, if it's all right to leave things behind." What did Gwydion miss? It didn't matter. The tension in the room clawed at him uncomfortably.

"Double check. If it's not sensitive or of sentimental value, if it can be replaced, leave it. Stay checked in." Starkad stood too. "Meet us in front of the hotel across the street in five."

Kirby didn't like the needles and pins feeling that coated her skin. It was made worse by the thought of Brit's convenient offer of *information* so soon before the atmosphere went sideways.

Starkad had called them a taxi, and she, he, and Gwydion were on their way to the airport. She hated that Starkad had to sit in the front seat due to space restraints, but she was next to Gwydion. Having both men nearby didn't eliminate the uncomfortable feeling, but it made her better equipped to deal with whatever was associated with this sensation.

Focus. She wouldn't get sucked into panic. What did data did she have? Gwydion seemed to understand *travel light.* He'd shown up with a single bag. If Min had been here, she suspected he'd have brought several pieces of luggage.

Then again, if he were here, they wouldn't need an airport. She and Starkad discussed just flying. He couldn't, but she and Gwydion could transport him. However, there was no way for them to guarantee they'd be unseen.

Focus. No one was talking. Smart. Nothing for the driver to overhear. But if he was listening in, they had bigger problems. Was Hel watching them closely enough to know they were leaving? Would she send someone to sidetrack them? If she did, they didn't have a plan of action, aside from acting on some probably fake information Brit gave Starkad.

And why wouldn't Brit just go away? Why did Kirby's heart still hurt every time she thought about her?

Focus. Get to the airport and check in with the boarding pass she had in her hand. She'd already checked in with two others online. This was *status quo* for all missions. When she, Starkad, and Gwydion were someplace private, they'd figure out next steps. Current step—make it safely to another country.

The sound of the engine stopped abruptly, leaving an empty space where the steady hum had been seconds earlier. Kirby shoved aside any rambling thoughts, and the world shifted to a hyper-real sharpness. The taxi was drifting to a stop, as the driver maneuvered them to the side of the road. There were no buildings within view. The landscape was mostly grass and trees. Their driver was cursing loudly and turning the key in the ignition over and over, with no result.

"Is there a problem?" Starkad's question was cool, carried on a hint of menace.

"I don't know. The car should be fine. Electrical fuck-up, I'm guessing." Each time the driver turned the key, there was a series of *clicks*, but nothing else. "I'll call for another car for you, so you won't miss your flight."

This wasn't right. Several of the gods dabbled in electricity, but not Hel. Not that Kirby knew of, anyway. The goddess hid ninety-nine percent of her power at the TOM academy, but Kirby remembered from her first life.

"If you want to stretch your legs or anything"—the driver was jabbing at his phone with a shaky hand—"I can have someone here in a few minutes."

"We'll do that," Starkad said. He was intimidating, but not typically *make people shake in their boots* scary unless he wanted to be. The driver was too nervous.

If something was going on, being outside was better than being stuck in a small box. Every tiny hair on Kirby's body stood on end, as they piled out onto the side of the road. They all had their bags slung over their shoulders. This type of operation required total mobility, rather than stashing things in trunks.

This respite could be a chance to plan. Many gods could teleport, but Kirby didn't know of any who could make themselves invisible. And if one could, would they isolate themselves out here, waiting?

Kirby would, if it meant getting her target. *Not comforting.*

The instant they closed the car doors, the taxi roared to life, and the driver pealed onto the road, leaving them in the dust. Literally.

"We should fly," Gwydion said, as he looked in every direction at once. "We should have done that to begin with. To the docks, perhaps. Take a boat. Those are easier to disembark than a plane."

"You two found her. I'm so glad." Loki's voice came from behind.

Kirby's stomach turned itself inside out. Her dagger was in her hand before she processed drawing it, and flame she didn't summon licked along the blade. She lunged at Loki. He disappeared before she reached him, appearing several meters behind her, but she expected it. She was already pivoting.

A familiar roar shredded the air. Kirby didn't need to look, to know Starkad had shifted. She hadn't seen him become a wolf in centuries, but she'd have to be awed later.

Freya, help me to make peace among my enemies. The familiar prayer echoed in Kirby's thoughts, and she gritted her teeth to shove it aside.

Starkad landed with his paws on Loki's shoulders, pinning him to the ground, but the god vanished again before Starkad could clamp his jaw around anything.

When Loki reappeared, roots and grass sprung from the ground, tangling around his limbs and causing him to stumble.

Kirby knew without looking the plant growth was Gwydion's doing. They didn't keep him from blinking out of sight again, but the plants offered valuable counter-attack time. She set an easy pattern with Starkad, the two of them taking turns attacking Loki without hesitation when he appeared. Keeping him on the defensive. She'd never fought with Starkad on a battlefield, but they'd sparred plenty across two lives, and time melted away now.

Loki fired a ball of lightning at Kirby, striking her in the chest and sending her stumbling back. Starkad darted in front of her, shielding her while she recovered, and Loki fired off more electricity.

The power singed and crackled along Starkad's fur. The scent of burning hair and flesh filled the air, making Kirby's eyes water. No time to pause. No time to be distracted. She spun toward the spark of magic to her right and slashed at Loki with her dagger.

For each successful hit Kirby or Starkad landed, Loki managed several of his own. The god was no longer blinking around as quickly, and exhaustion shone on his face.

But Starkad was panting, and strain ached over every inch of Kirby. Could they outlast Loki?

He phased again, this time coming up behind Gwydion and locking him in place as a shield. "I'm not here to fight, idiots." Loki spoke through clenched teeth.

Could Kirby shoot through Gwydion? No. Any attack meant to hurt Loki would do the same to Gwydion. "Uh-huh."

"At least the *don't believe anything* part of your indoctrination stuck." Loki rolled his eyes. "I've never been your enemy."

Kirby snorted with laughter. "You recruited me, knowing who I was. You helped sentence me."

"Starkad knew who you were, too. And Hel sentenced you. I didn't care one way or the other."

Because apathy was so much better than antipathy. This conversation gave her more time to look for an opening, but Loki had to know she would. What was he stalling for? "If you're not here to fight, what do you want?" she asked.

She felt Starkad tense. He wasn't touching her or in sight; the sensation washed through her. He was preparing to attack, while she distracted Loki.

"Brit lied to you about Hel's weakness. About the fire," Loki said.

Starkad lunged at Loki.

Kirby extended a force field to wrap around Gwydion and remove him from the equation.

"If you don't want my help, good luck on your own," Loki said. As Starkad clenched his jaw around Loki's throat, Loki vanished.

"Is he gone?" Kirby asked. She knew the answer. Unlike all the blinking around the battlefield he'd done, this time when he blinked out of sight, the layers of anxiety she'd felt all morning faded too. The adrenaline rushed from her veins, and she sank to her knees as exhaustion took over.

Starkad collapsed next to her on the ground, on his side, panting for breath. He looked exactly the way she remembered—his body shape had shifted enough to tear most of his clothing, with the muscle changing under his skin and fur growing on top. He'd stayed mostly bi-pedal, but his leg structure shifted to something more canine, and his head had became mostly wolfish. It was fierce and beautiful. He managed a grunt. He could speak in this form, but not well.

She stroked a hand along his jaw and glided her fingers through his fur. He was fading back to human, which meant he didn't sense a threat either.

Brit lied. Story of Kirby's life.

"Are you both all right?" Gwydion knelt next to them, his gaze on her.

"Feeling a bit out of practice." Starkad's words were as much growl as English.

Brit lied. Old news. Kirby needed to move past it. It was just as possible Loki was lying. Regardless, he said what he did, to deceive. To encase them in doubt and make them question every step they took and every decision they made. His offers of *help* were no more genuine than Brit's, or he'd still be here.

Gwydion sat. "What now?"

Kirby dropped to her butt and crossed her legs. They could walk back into town. Call for another ride. Do what Gwydion suggested and fly to the docks. "We don't know how they keep finding us. Have they really known all this time and let it ride, even when we were taking out their assassins?"

"No." Starkad was human again, rolled onto his back. Scorch marks decorated his chest and arms, where Loki's lightning had struck. "Someone is telling them."

It was a mistake to linger in town last night. Not that Kirby minded the results, but now... "Who?"

"No one here," Gwydion said.

That was comforting because she believed it. It was nice that something could be. But it still didn't answer the question of, *what next?*

CHAPTER TWENTY

Starkad ached in places he'd forgotten could hurt. That was in addition to the burns across his torso and arms. He was healing, but not as quickly as he usually did. Loki left more than a couple new scars.

Starkad lay next to Kirby on the hard ground, staring up at the clear sky. Strength hummed through him. It had been a long time since he felt this alive. A fight like the one they'd just been in was exhilarating. His beast paced inside him, and the sharpness lingered in his senses. He swore he could taste Kirby without even touching her.

The wolf inside wanted to go pick another fight. To find a god or other immortal to throw down with until he was battered and exhausted.

The human bit—the part that had kept him acceptable in polite society for the last couple centuries—knew they had more important things to focus on.

Once those were done, he'd be standing in front of Hel. Then he could fight.

"We could go back to Aeval." Gwydion's voice was strained. He hadn't enjoyed this as much, but he was all right, anyway. He made Kirby smile.

Starkad warred with the balance between primitive instinct and more rational thought. "Can we be certain she's not the one who sold us out to Hel?"

"I trust her, but if you don't, look at it this way—it's similar to how you approach the things Loki tells you," Gwydion said.

Kirby raised her brows. "We acknowledge he's an insane sadist and approach accordingly? Aeval was a little manic, but she wasn't even in the same realm."

"You can't second-guess every person you meet, or you'll be stuck in the limbo of never trusting anyone. She's never given me a reason not to, so we trust her now." Gwydion stood and offered Kirby a hand up. "Besides, her place is only a few kilometers away, and I could go for some of that *best coffee ever*."

Starkad forced himself to stand. It wasn't that he was too tired—most of the aches were nagging jabs by now—but the rest wanted to hunch down and race between the trees. To hide and hunt.

"It's a good next step," Starkad agreed. He'd only met Aeval a few times, but he'd never taken issue with her.

They all changed into intact clothing and stashed their tattered rags.

They walked in mostly silence. Starkad wanted to focus on questions and next steps. He had to move past the roaring voice in his head, whose answer to everything was, *Hunt. Kill. Destroy.*

Kirby strolled between him and Gwydion, close enough that her arm brushed Starkad's.

As they neared town, the acrid scents of smoke and burning wood singed his sinuses. That wasn't a cooking smell; flesh and iron were mixed in.

Kirby and Gwydion paused, twitching their noses. In unspoken agreement, the three broke into a flat run in the direction of the heavy black cloud in the sky.

When they reached a narrow road with a building gutted by an explosion, Starkad didn't have to ask, to know it was Aeval's coffee shop.

Emergency crews were on the scene, digging though rubble and holding people back.

"This looks like the bookstore in London." Hurt and disbelief rang in Kirby's words.

It was worse. Starkad couldn't ignore the stench. "Multiple someones were caught in this one."

"No." Aeval's voice came from behind. "They were taken away from here before everything was destroyed."

They spun to find her standing on the sidewalk with the other onlookers. Fury and grief distorted her face.

Gwydion reached for her, and she fell into his arms with a heavy sigh. She stood there for a moment, face buried in his chest and body shaking.

A glance at Kirby said she was worried, not jealous. "What happened?"

Aeval extracted herself from Gwydion's comfort, and focused on Kirby instead. "They stormed the building. Soldiers in black and iron. The metal scorched my people's flesh. The intruders pinned us down and knocked me out. When I came to, my people were being hauled out in shackles, their skin still smoking, and the building was burning around me."

"They left you here for us to find." Starkad was struggling to stay human. To show sympathy appropriately. Solider and berserker wanted to go *now*. To find the threat.

Aeval was looking at Kirby. "Do you remember when I said your justice clashes with mine?"

Kirby nodded.

"I will give you whatever you need— information, safety, money. Bring my people home to me. I'd prefer alive, but if not, let me put their bodies to rest. Find justice. For me. For us. For everyone TOM has done this to." Rage dripped from Aeval's words and sparked in the air around her. Dark clouds moved in overhead.

Kirby nodded again. "We're trying."

A few drops of rain struck the ground, and then dozens more. Fat, wet, and unusually warm for the region, as though the sky wept.

Aeval pressed a key into Gwydion's palm. "This will take you to safety. To my court. It will give you time to regroup and plan. Stay until you're ready, then come back here and obliterate Hel and all those who follow TOM."

"We will." Starkad reveled in the growl in his words. The fur on the back of his neck soaked up the rain.

The skies opened up and poured water down. The storm was Aeval's, washing away the darkness that lingered in the area.

They might not know how to destroy Hel, but Starkad could be torn to shreds again and again until the job was done, and the beast inside would enjoy every minute of it.

Kirby plucked the key from Gwydion's hand and held it up, letting water cling to it. The ancient silver design cast a faint glow, creating a million tiny rainbows. "How does it—"

She vanished, and the key clattered to the sidewalk.

Starkad stopped fighting the beast and roared into the storm. Where was Kirby?

Brit stared at the clock on the hotel-room nightstand. Had she really slept for ten hours? She didn't feel rested, but she also didn't remember tossing and turning from bad dreams.

What came before was fuzzy, too. Hel telling her to prove her loyalty? Brit had been careful. No one knew she'd been feeding information to Starkad. She'd completely hidden that this was her last mission. That she intended to leave.

That wasn't right. Her head throbbed with conflicting memories. She'd already left. None of it went the way she planned. Kirby—

"Afternoon, Sleeping Beauty." Mark's dry tone cut through her confusion.

Bile rose in Brit's throat, and she focused on him. He was supposed to be dead. No, that wasn't right. The mission had gone wrong this morning. Her shoulder throbbed with the reminder of a grenade dislocating it.

"Hey," she croaked out, keeping the confusion from her face.

"You still up for cake?" Mark sat on the bed next to her and brushed her hair from her face. It didn't matter that his touch was gentle; it still sent revulsion racing through her.

She nodded, not trusting her memories or emotions enough to say much. He was supposed to be dead. She'd shot him in the back of the head.

"Are you certain you're up for it? I can order something in if you'd prefer." Mark sounded so kind. Actually concerned for her welfare.

Brit knew better; he'd never been worried about her. Why didn't he have a hole in the back of his head? She struggled to sit, and her shoulder screamed in protest when she put her weight on it.

"Take it easy." Mark had a hand behind her back in an instant, keeping her from falling back and helping her to sit.

She bit the inside of her cheek, to keep from screaming. In pain or frustration, she wasn't sure. She refused his help in the shower, especially when he offered too sweetly. As they headed out to the car, the past solidified in her head. They'd been here on a mission, and Kirby stopped them. She was alive.

Of course she is.

That didn't make sense. Brit had been told years ago that Kirby killed herself. She shook the confusion aside. It didn't become clear until this morning that Kirby was still among the living. And Mark had gotten special permission for them to stay and hunt her, after she disrupted their current mission.

Kirby was responsible for killing their teammates. The ones Brit had pointed Starkad too.

The pain pills Mark gave her must be fucking with her head, but the drive to the cake place helped her sort everything. By the time they arrived, she knew where she was and what she needed to be doing.

The bakery looked more like a diner, with menus and booths, but that didn't surprise Brit. Why not? She'd never been here before. An image whispered through her thoughts. If she looked toward the back, would she see a familiar god?

She didn't know any gods except Hel and Loki, so probably not.

"Are you all right?" Mark asked. "You're a little out of it."

"Having a hard time, shaking the pain pills." This time her smile came easily. She was the best sniper TOM had, but she was also exceptional at masking whatever lurked inside her head and heart.

His phone rang, and he excused himself to take the call outside. If he was moving away from prying ears, it was mission related. He'd fill her in later.

She waited impatiently for his return. "Hello, partner," Kirby whispered in her ear, pressing into her from behind. "It's been too long."

This was familiar. Intensely close and intimate.

Brit's fingers twitched with the instinct of reaching for her gun. With her right arm in a sling, there was no way she'd get any sort of drop on Kirby. Not that she wanted to. An apology stuck in her throat. The desire to beg for forgiveness.

Shoot her. The scream in Brit's head was in her own voice. *Someone's watching.*

That sounded like a good reason to not shoot Kirby. The alley was empty, though. No one was back here except them.

Her body remembered this closeness and begged her to grind back into Kirby. Phantom want mingled with her growing nausea. "You sound and feel incredible, for a ghost," Brit said.

"And I look much better than you do."

"Always a matter of opinion."

Shoot her. The instinct made her ears ring, drowning out Kirby's words as she and Brit headed outside.

Brit's gut was flipping in on itself. She didn't want to kill Kirby. That was the last thing she wanted.

Shoot her.

Brit elbowed Kirby in the gut with her left arm.

Kirby grunted.

Shooting her is the only way to save her.

The thought didn't make sense, but Brit believed it in her core. She pushed past the pain, whirled, and grabbed Kirby's gun. She didn't hesitate to level off the sights and pull the trigger.

The bullet caught Kirby in the chest, and she landed on her back, disbelief splashed across her face.

Grief welled up inside Brit.

Swallow it.

"The fuck?" Mark was standing next to her. "Nice job. Drop her gun. We need to go now."

Brit couldn't go with the smug-faced asshole who had tortured her for years. Who beat and raped her. Who blamed her for being frigid. "No."

"Excuse me?"

Her shoulder roared in agony. If she could make it work, one more shot wouldn't matter. She swallowed the pain, raised her arm again, and shot him in the head.

Now he was dead. Lying on the ground next to Kirby. He was *actually* dead this time. She could see the blood, pooling from his skull. Seeping into her shoes.

Brit needed to get out of here, before the police arrived. Before the pain overwhelmed her. Darkness licked at the edges of her vision. She stepped back from the blood, and kicked off her shoes when she was clear of the puddle.

Her legs wobbled, and her world went black.

Brit stared at the clock on the hotel-room nightstand. Had she really slept for ten hours? She didn't feel rested, but she also didn't remember tossing and turning from bad dreams.

What came before was fuzzy, too. Hel telling her to prove her loyalty? Brit had been careful. No one knew she'd been feeding information to Starkad. She'd completely hidden that this was her last mission. That she intended to leave.

That wasn't right. Her head throbbed with conflicting memories. She'd already left. None of it went the way she planned. Kirby—

"Afternoon, Sleeping Beauty." Mark's dry tone cut through her confusion.

Bile rose in Brit's throat, and she swallowed the desire to vomit on him. She wasn't going through this again.

He drew within arm's reach.

She pushed past the haze and the pain, grabbed his gun from his holster, and shot him. She emptied the magazine into his chest and head, still squeezing the trigger after she ran out of bullets.

He was gone this time. Unlike when she'd shot him and neglected to check. Bits of him stuck to the comforter and the walls.

Brit needed to get out of here before someone called the police. Darkness flooded in, and her world faded to black.

"Afternoon, Sleeping Beauty."

The creeping hints of madness echoed in Brit's skull, threatening to tear from her throat, and she turned to look at Mark.

CHAPTER TWENTY-ONE

Kirby landed on her back on the ground, staring up at the sky. She couldn't move, but she hadn't been in control of her body since she arrived. One second she'd been on the sidewalk next to Starkad, Gwydion, and Aeval, and the next she was standing behind Brit in the gourmet cake shop.

It didn't matter that Kirby knew these events had already transpired; she said and did everything exactly like she originally had.

Up until Brit shot her.

"The fuck?" Mark's voice chilled her. He was supposed to be dead. "Nice job. Drop her gun. We need to go now."

Kirby tried to turn her head to look at him. She couldn't. There was a gaping hole in her, and she didn't feel any of it. The one thing that hurt was the look on Brit's face when she shot Kirby.

"No," Brit said.

Mark's arm moved into view. "Excuse me?"

More gunshots rang out. Someone would hear. Why weren't there people running back here?

She saw the splash of clothing and color, as Mark fell past her line of sight. Though she didn't feel it, she knew he lay on the ground next to her.

This wasn't right. Kirby had lived through this. Gwydion had found her a few minutes later. And Mark had choked her out. Brit was too hurt to shoot her. Was sorry she hadn't done more. Had tried in her own way to earn Kirby's forgiveness since.

Kirby's world went black, and she was standing behind Brit again. "Hello, partner," Kirby whispered in Brit's ear, pressing into her from behind. "It's been too long."

It didn't matter how many times the scene replayed, Kirby couldn't make herself act differently. She was confined to the same actions with each repeat. Sometimes Brit shot her first. Sometimes Mark strangled her, and then Brit planted a bullet in her head or chest.

Kirby died over and over. At least, unlike with her past lives, she didn't feel the pain of dying. But she felt Brit's loathing. The hatred and disgust that hung in her gaze, every time she looked at Kirby.

After a dozen times, Kirby lost count. There must have been more than a hundred in total. Thousands? Why was this happening? Who had thrown her into this nightmare?

Still Brit's sneering face looked down on her after each death.

Why did Kirby let her live? Why did she think Brit could ever atone? Brit didn't care about Kirby, beyond proving that Brit was better. And now she had.

Mark approached, as Kirby held Brit prisoner. With a sweep of his feet under hers, Kirby was on her back again, this time without a bullet hole in her. He wedged a knee between her legs and pressed a hand to her throat. "The three of us would have been good together."

Brit was supposed to shoot him now. Kirby didn't care if she got blood and brains on her. She couldn't move. This wasn't supposed to happen this way.

Mark ripped at her shirt, leaving her exposed, as he leered down at her.

A sob welled in Kirby's throat. Why couldn't she fight back? Why was Brit just watching?

He tore at her jeans, ripping them away. Denim didn't shred that way—like paper. This wasn't right. It wasn't fair.

Did Brit hate her so much that she was just going to stand there?

Kirby reached as deep as she could, digging inside to wake up from this twisted fucking dream. She grasped something else. The same thing she'd found when Hel pinned her to the pillar.

That seemed like an eternity ago.

Kirby could see Mark's holster. The idiot had left his gun unsecured, like he always did. The douchenozzle thought he was impervious. A mental yell echoed in her head, as she forced her fingers to move. Just a twitch.

He didn't see, but Brit's gaze drifted to Kirby's hand.

Kirby didn't care. The invisible restraints shattered. She grabbed Mark's gun, leveled it off, and squeezed the trigger.

As he slumped, she rolled, came up on one knee, and aimed at Brit. She wasn't fast enough—Brit had a bead on her.

The gunshot echoed in Kirby's ears, and she landed on her back. Again. Staring at the sky, unable to move.

The cake shop vanished. About fucking time.

Kirby strained to hold onto the control she'd captured moments earlier.

"I'm proud of you." That was Hel.

Kirby's world swirled into view, and she was in Hel's office at the academy.

Hel wasn't talking to her, though.

Brit strolled past, as if Kirby wasn't there. "I told you, I only want to serve you. Whatever it takes to prove my loyalty."

"And you have." Hel cradled Brit's cheek. "You've done so very well."

Brit stood in front of Hel, hundreds of iterations of the showdown in Salt Lake clashing in her head. This was reality. She had no doubt. Now that she was conscious, she recognized that the fucked up *Groundhog's Day* was Hel's trial. Killing Kirby over and over was Brit's proof that she could turn against the one person she loved, to serve Hel.

"How long has it been?" Brit needed to fill in the blanks, to solidify herself in the real world. It felt like months had passed.

"For you? Weeks. But only a few seconds to the rest of the world." Hel studied her.

Fear should be raging inside, but Brit was numb. Killing Mark over and over, only to have him come back, had shredded her stomach. Shooting Kirby repeatedly destroyed her heart. Whatever gave her the presence of mind to do so... That was an instinct she didn't want to touch ever again. If she thought she hated herself before, it was nothing compared to now.

Kirby's cold, lifeless eyes would haunt Brit for the rest of her life. If she was lucky, that wouldn't be much longer.

Her terror of Hel was gone, though. Brit had sampled damnation, and there was no physical pain that could be worse.

"You did the one thing Kirby never did." Hel's tone was kind.

"What's that?"

Hel smiled. "You killed Mark. I waited for so long, for her to take that initiative. To destroy that part of her torment. She was too weak."

"You let him walk around, in the hopes that someone would murder him?"

"Specifically Kirby."

Brit should be angry about that, but it wasn't a surprise. "Why?"

"There were aspects of her that needed to be broken. And they were, just not in the way I hoped. When Starkad took her out of here, we thought we'd pushed too hard. But she was dead. If we couldn't break her—make her ours—at least the threat was removed."

Now Brit was angry. It was almost enough to shatter her mask. "Oh?"

Hel shrugged. "It doesn't matter any longer. You changed everything. You're so much stronger than she is, and it's a shame you weren't born with her gifts."

Brit wouldn't get sucked into the praise she'd longed to hear for more than a decade. This was the recognition she'd always wanted, and it tasted foul.

"Will you fight beside me, to destroy her?" Hel asked. "Can you?"

"Yes." Brit had just executed the woman she loved hundreds of times. And once Kirby saw her by Hel's side, Brit would never be forgiven. But her agreement was a lie. Whatever came next, as long as it gave Brit the chance to stab Hel in the back when the time came, the sacrifice was worth it.

Hel lifted Brit's chin, forcing Brit to meet her gaze. "I'm going to give you the gift she wasted. As my servant, you'll have immortality for as long as your loyalty lasts."

That sounded sucky. No surprise there. "I'm your servant until you deem me done or no longer worthy."

"Excellent."

The first sparks across Brit's skin tingled. An insignificant irritation. The electricity grew, jolting through her every joint and nerve ending. Swelling, until the pain was nothing like she'd ever experienced. Until she couldn't help but let the agony rip from her throat in a ragged scream.

And then it was over. Hel dropped her hand but didn't move away.

Brit suspected that didn't have to hurt, especially not that much.

"One more thing," Hel said, as if it was an afterthought. "You weren't the only one who lived through that. I let Kirby join you. That was actually her. If it were an option, I'd lock her there permanently, but making her live the torment repeatedly was pleasant."

Brit mentally clenched her fists, unable to fight the image of executing Hel over and over, the same way she had Kirby. She never let the reaction show. "Good." Her own response threatened to make her vomit. "I hope it fucked with her head."

"I do adore you." Hel's smile grew. "Let's go." The office vanished, and they were standing on a tiny street, across from Gwydion, a terrifying wolf-like creature, and a furious Kirby.

Someone was about to die.

Please let it be Hel, and let it be horrific.

CHAPTER TWENTY-TWO

Kirby reappeared on the street by Aeval's destroyed coffee shop. The emergency crews were gone. Everyone was gone, except Gwydion, Aeval, and Starkad—who was in berserker form again.

What happened?

The question lodged in her throat, stuck on days and months of relived betrayal. Her heart ached at the memories. At Brit's coldness. At the memory of being shot again and again.

Starkad's growl forced her attention to where Hel and Brit stood just a few meters away.

All-consuming rage pumped through Kirby, and she drew her dagger. She shouted and charged Hel, flame licking along her blade.

Brit stepped between Kirby and the goddess. The temptation to focus on Brit instead of Hel made Kirby's step falter. She needed to take out the primary target.

Starkad dodged in front of her, jaws snapping as he locked them on Brit's throat.

Kirby forced herself forward, continuing on her path to Hel. *Please let the fire work.* She and Starkad might be on their own in this fight, since the stone ground would limit Gwydion's power, so this needed to be effective.

She heard the scrape of claws on stone, and instinct wanted her to look at Starkad. The distraction was enough for Hel. An invisible force pinned Kirby to a nearby wall.

Kirby struggled against the magical bonds. She knew how to break them. She'd done it before.

The stone shattered around Hel's feet, rock shrapnel flying at the goddess as roots climbed from beneath the ground.

The hold on Kirby vanished, and she dropped to her feet. A quick glance at Gwydion showed him and Aeval with their faces drawn and a soft glow surrounding them.

Kirby gave her full attention to Hel, who was struggling against vines and tree roots that grew faster than she could freeze them. Kirby slashed with the fiery blade, catching Hel's clothing, and Hel flung a spiked ball at her. The ice slammed into Kirby's chest and sent her stumbling as she struggled to catch her breath.

Out of the corner of her eye, she saw Brit draw a gun. *Fucking idiot.* That hadn't worked on Starkad last time. Today wouldn't be any different.

Brit squeezed the trigger, and Starkad jerked back with a yelp. Blood spilled from a fresh wound in his shoulder. What the fuck?

A series of tree branches wrapped around Brit, preventing her from shooting again.

Kirby's Valkyrie armor closed in around her. The summoned protection was familiar and right. As she lunged toward Hel again, a series of ice balls bounced off the transparent shield.

This was nothing like fighting Loki. He'd gone on the defensive, blinking from one spot to the next, but Hel was pushing in. Looking for any opening and exploiting every weakness.

Gwydion shouted in pain. Kirby knew better than to look. She slashed at Hel, ducking and weaving under each attack. She was avoiding being hit, but she wasn't landing any strikes either. Starkad roared in pain, and it took all of Kirby's willpower to stay focused on her own fight.

Hel pierced Kirby's magical shield and sent an ice spear through her calf.

Kirby stumbled, jolting herself when she fell on her knee. Another gunshot rang in her ears.

Brit had fired again.

Starkad's load roar shredded Kirby's soul. He might not be able to die, but he could be hurt. She could almost feel his pain.

Kirby needed to get to Hel. Once the goddess was gone, they could deal with cleanup. The branches growing around Hel shattered into a million icy pieces. They lined up in a spiked wall and flew at Hel. That had to be Gwydion.

They burned away to ash, fluttering uselessly to the ground before they reached her.

Shock and despair filled Kirby.

Hel barked a laugh. "Yes, I wield fire, too. I suppose you weren't expecting that."

Brit lied.

244

Kirby charged toward Hel, crouched low and dagger forward.

Brit lied

Behind her, another shot rang through the air, and Starkad howled in pain.

Brit lied

Gwydion's branches and Aeval's vines wilted and withered before they could wrap around Hel.

Hel summoned another spear of ice and threw.

It caught Kirby in the upper thigh, and she stumbled, her hip slamming into the ground. Hopelessness licked her senses. She tried to push back the edges of despair, but did they have any hope of winning this fight?

Min knocked on Daz's door. The faint whisper of smoke greeted him when Daz answered. Odd thing to smell in a hotel room.

"I'm going out for brunch, if you'd like to keep me company," Min said. It was preferable to sitting in his room, wondering, *what next*?

Daz grinned. "Brunch sounds delightful. Let me grab the keys."

"We'll walk…" Min trailed off when Daz turned away, revealing more of the room behind him. Faint wisps of smoke rose from the wastebasket by the desk. "What's that?"

Daz glanced over his shoulder. His cheer wilted. "Nothing." He moved in front of Min. "Walking would be wonderful."

Min saw the scorched and mostly burned remnants of his letter to Kirby in the trash. The paper and two envelops, in addition to the *K* in his handwriting on a scrap of paper, gave it away.

"You need to move on," Daz said. "Kirby will be gone soon, this time for good if you're lucky, so you can finally live your life for you."

Fury licked Min's senses. He didn't remember the last time he'd summoned his full power, but it spilled into his veins without effort now. He whirled on the god he'd called *friend and confidant* for decades. "What did you do?"

Daz's eyes grew wide. "I looked out for you. The way I always have."

"What did you do?" Min stepped toward him.

"I don't care who you love." Daz backed away. "I know it will never be me. But she destroys you. You're a shell because of her. I've given you riches and success, and you can enjoy them."

"*What did you do?*" Min's question rattled the walls and windows.

"Now that she's immortal, truly returned to her original form, Hel knows how to keep her from coming back." Daz's voice wavered. "By this time tomorrow, she'll be gone for good. Hel promised me—"

Min roared, his rage fueled by the deep crack running through his heart, and Daz was incinerated. The ashes fluttered in the streams of light coming through the windows.

Was this the same feeling that drove Kirby? This all-consuming desire to see someone suffer? If so, he finally understood. He would destroy anyone who interfered with his life or hers.

He dialed Gwydion as he headed to the main floor of the hotel. No answer. It was the same with Starkad's and Kirby's numbers. Where were they? If Daz gave Hel a location, it was the hotel Min left them in.

This was one of those instances where it would have been nice to be able to fly.

In the lobby, he tracked down a valet attendant. "What do we have in the lot that's fast, small, and not limited edition?"

"Uh... we have a BMW Z4."

Min grabbed the keys. "Reimburse the guest. Give them my apology," he called over his shoulder as he headed to the garage. A perk of owning the hotel—he could tell the staff what to do, and had the money to cover this extravagance.

He hit the main streets with rubber spinning on asphalt, and floored the gas as soon as he was clear of traffic. By the time he reached the city limits, he had buried the needle.

Please let me get to them in time. He didn't know who the prayer was to, but it better be someone more powerful than he was.

CHAPTER TWENTY-THREE

Kirby snapped off both ends of the spear sticking through her leg. She screamed in pain at the ice that clawed through her, as her body tried to heal around the magical remnants of the melted weapon. Hel assaulted her with a barrage of icicles. Most bounced off Kirby's magical shield, but a few penetrated, nicking her skin before evaporating.

Starkad was on all fours on the ground, blood flowing freely from wounds she couldn't see from this angle. Aeval lay unconscious on the stone. At least, Kirby hoped she was still breathing. The branches Gwydion summoned were thinner with each wave.

The squealing of tires split the air. What now?

A BMW skidded to a stop at the edge of the battlefield, and Min climbed out.

Fucker. Kirby wanted to be angry at him for coming back now, but she'd expended all her rage on Brit.

A wash of power spilled from him, rolling across the ground. It soothed Kirby, wrapping her in a love and adoration she didn't want to feel. It knocked Hel back a few feet.

Kirby was moving again, Starkad by her side, before Hel regained her balance. Why wasn't Brit stopping him? It didn't matter.

Hel flung out a fireball that struck Gwydion in the chest, and he stumbled. A second attack from her blasted Starkad back, and she turned her attention toward Kirby, driving at her with another spear.

Brit stepped behind Hel, and light shimmered around her, coalescing in a scythe. The fuck? That was new. Brit swung and buried the blade in Hel's back.

Hel whirled on Brit with a roar. "I warned you not to betray me." She back-handed Brit, who crumpled in a pile, unmoving.

Kirby was already running forward again, taking advantage of the distraction. She swung, and her dagger seemed to grow almost a meter. She sliced through Hel's neck, sending the goddess's head rolling.

Flame licked off Kirby, fueled by power from someone behind her and burning Hel's body to cinders. "See you in another life, bitch," Kirby spat.

Numbness swam in, and she landed on her butt. Was it really over?

Min stepped in front of her, and she turned away. He wasn't a priority. She needed to know if Starkad and Gwydion were all right. Aeval too.

They were all staggering to their feet, making their way toward her. Min was by her side again. "I came to warn you," he said. "I'm sorry I didn't arrive sooner."

"Yeah, okay." Kirby was too tired to engage him. All her energy was gone.

"Take care of yourself and your lovers," Min stepped back. "I'll abide by my promise to leave."

And then Starkad was next to her, on all fours and nuzzling her hand. She ran her palms over his chest. Blood matted his fur, but the holes were healing.

Gwydion knelt next to her and crushed his mouth to hers.

Kirby wanted to scream and laugh and cry. Hel was gone. Brit was gone. An ugly chapter in her life was over.

And she'd celebrate and mourn when she could think again.

Kirby let consciousness seep in slowly and reached out for one of two familiar forms that should be flanking her in the bed. Her hand met empty, wrinkled sheets. She frowned and rolled onto her other side, reluctant to open her eyes. No one else was here.

She surrendered to the idea of being awake and sat up. The room was something straight out of a fairy tale. Or a catalog. She was in a large bed with feather-soft sheets and comforter, surrounded by gauzy curtains. The ornate, wood furniture was part of the vision, rather than disrupting it. And the softest light spilled through a large window.

How late had she slept? Enough that most of the aches from the battle with Hel had vanished. Was it really only yesterday? It felt both like an eternity ago, and like the memory would never soften.

They'd confirmed Brit was dead. Kirby didn't know how she felt about it. So much betrayal couldn't be corrected with a single act of sacrifice, even if Brit's attack on Hel had helped turn the tide of the battle.

Or was it Min's arrival that changed things? Kirby hated how cheesy the notion was, but it seemed as though his passion and love of life were the counterbalance to Hel's lust for destruction.

Kirby didn't understand why, but he said he'd take care of Brit's arrangements. He'd left without argument. Surprising, but pleasantly respectful of her wishes.

She followed her nose toward the scent of fresh coffee, and found Gwydion and Starkad in the kitchen. It was impossible to fight her smile. "Morning."

"Early afternoon." Gwydion set a mug of coffee in front of her. "But we're not keeping track."

Another thing to be grateful for—a short respite from the fight. And the coffee was good. Not Aeval-good, though the fae queen was responsible for their current living quarters. She'd set them up with a cottage in her little realm of fairies, and said they were welcome anytime. Then she left, to take care of things in her kingdom.

Starkad had explained to Kirby that yesterday, when Brit was killing her over and over, she'd only been gone for a few seconds in real life.

251

Enough time for them to know Hel was around, and for Gwydion and Aeval to fuzz the lines of reality to separate them from the people on the streets.

When the fight was over, the illusion faded, leaving destroyed sidewalks and roads visible to everyone. But people didn't like to see what they didn't understand, and most of them easily accepted that the destruction was part of the explosion that took out Aeval's coffee shop.

Kirby sipped her coffee and enjoyed the serenity.

Starkad's features were sharper than yesterday. His berserker lingered closer to the surface. She could feel it, pacing inside him. It was comforting.

Gwydion almost glowed. He seemed closer to the ambient magic in centuries.

And Kirby… She felt more complete than she had at any point in this short life. Pieces were still missing. Holes caused by her time with TOM. An ache she couldn't define and didn't know how to soothe. But she'd take *better than yesterday* any day.

Starkad's phone chirped.

"That thing works in here?" Kirby was surprised.

Gwydion took a seat at the wooden table. "It'd be hard to communicate with the outside world if it didn't."

Wasn't that the point? Kirby's questions evaporated when a frown spread across Starkad's face.

He slid her the phone. "It's from Brit. For you." His tone was grim. "I'll delete it if you'd prefer."

Kirby's chill shriveled into a pile of ash. "No. I want to see it." She pulled up the encrypted message, timestamped right after Brit had called Starkad with the lie about Hel's weakness.

A video loaded, and Brit's face filled the screen. Impassive and cool, like always. "Hey." Her voice was jarring in its sweetness. "I'm not quite sure what to say. I should probably make this short. I hope you're seeing my message, because if you're not, Hel is still alive. You're going to think I sided with her. I hope you do, because I need her to believe the same. I hope the fire thing works for you. I got the information from some guy who called himself Daz."

Brit breathed out a long sigh, and static crackled over the speakers. "I don't know if what I'm doing is right, but it feels like it. For the first time in forever, this is scary but it feels like what needs to be done. I don't expect you to believe me or forgive me. I do have information for you, though. Hel's death will trigger the delivery of this message. It's linked to the same dead man's switch that will set other things into motion. The Campus Police at TOM academy are making arrangements to destroy the school. Anyone at the school who Hel didn't deem *converted* be dead in the next six months."

Kirby was going to be ill. They'd kill all those students?

"And a series of orders will go out to all of their field agents. Every assassin will be sent after a list of targets. Things are about to escalate," Brit said. "I'm attaching what I know. I can't say how much of it has changed. If anyone can ease the damage, you can. I know you won't buy what I'm saying—I don't expect you to—but I have to say it anyway. I'm sorry. And I really do love you."

Kirby gaped in disbelief as the message ended. What was she supposed to do with this information? "I don't understand." She didn't realize she was speaking aloud, until her voice hit her own ears. "This wasn't her. She didn't sacrifice…"

"She didn't just love you. She also wanted to be you," Gwydion said.

No. That was twisted and fucked up and wrong. And Kirby's life was the last thing that should be used as a template.

"It seems like she'd figured out what that meant," Starkad added.

That hurt more than Kirby wanted it to. "But I wouldn't—"

"Sacrifice everything for the person you loved?" Starkad covered her hand.

Kirby didn't want the burden of someone else looking up to her that way. Why couldn't Brit have been herself, selfish and oblivious, up until the end? She'd be alive and out of Kirby's life, and Kirby wouldn't have an old-new set of luggage to deal with. "I'll amend my previous statement. I don't want to understand."

Gwydion sighed. "Right there with you. But we still have to decide what to do with the information she gave you about TOM…"

Starkad took the phone back and scrolled through something. "It won't take much to confirm some of this. We can't let it slide. Dozens of people will die if it's true."

"I know." Kirby wished she didn't. It would be so much easier to ignore the reality. "We can't be everywhere at once."

"No, but we don't have to do this alone. Urd has resources," Starkad said.

Kirby wasn't used to that. Sure, he was always by her side, but an entire organization that was partially hidden in shadows? Could she trust them?

You can't second-guess every person you meet, or you'll be stuck in the limbo of never trusting anyone. Gwydion's words echoed in her head.

Things weren't done yet, even with Hel gone. Kirby, Starkad, and Gwydion... and perhaps Min, needed all the help they could get.

EPILOGUE

Min laid Brit's body on the mortuary table. It hurt, to walk away from Kirby again, but he finally understood and respected her wishes. He also had a lot of atoning to do. What happened with Daz was his fault. He'd been blind to so much, when it came to those in his life.

Anubis studied Brit's face, hovering a hand over her but not making contact. "Why bring her here? She's not one of yours. Or any of ours."

"She's defied her gods." The way Kirby did so long ago. In a way so few people ever had the strength to do. "But she deserves better than to be left forgotten in an unmarked grave."

Min had seen Brit's sacrifice. He would have assumed it was a last-minute change of heart, but Gwydion told him about the video Kirby received.

Anubis nodded and donned an apron. "Was she a solider?"

"Yes."

There was little to be done for Brit, but this would have to do. The room was as generic as most mortuaries, but power radiate from every crack. Stainless steel and tile everywhere. Easy to hose down and sterilize. The table Brit lay on was no different. If Brit's soul hadn't evaporated into the void—and chances were good it hadn't, based on her will in life—interring her as a soldier with Anubis' blessing would grant her some peace in the beyond.

"Would you like to assist?" Anubis asked.

Min and Brit loved the same woman, and both made mistakes when it came to their feelings. He felt an odd sort of kinship, with this person he barely knew. He put on an apron. "Yes."

Anubis grabbed a pair of large shears, started at the collar of Brit's tattered shirt, and cut down to remove the bloody top.

Brit gasped, and her eyes flew open. She sat straight up, hands over the hole in her gut. "Kirby?" Her voice was raspy.

"Alive." Min had never seen anything like this before.

"Hel?"

"Dead."

Brit exhaled noisily and collapsed back on the table with a loud *clang*. "Me?" Her question was barely a whisper.

Anubis passed his hand over her again, moving down her chest and lingering over the rapidly closing hole in her middle. The shock and confusion on his face matched what Min felt.

"I don't know what you are," Anubis said.